SAINT THÉRÈSE AND THE ROSES

SAINT THÉRÈSE

and the Roses

Written by Helen Walker Homan

Illustrated by George W. Thompson

IGNATIUS PRESS   SAN FRANCISCO

Cover design by Riz Boncan Marsella
Cover illustration by Christopher J. Pelicano

Published by Ignatius Press, San Francisco, 1995
All rights reserved
ISBN 0–89870–520–7
Library of Congress catalogue number 94–78941
Printed in the United States of America

CONTENTS

I

FRENCH LACE AND FINE JEWELS

LITTLE THÉRÈSE sat on the floor at her mother's feet, watching the bright needle as it flew through the cloud of fine lace her mother was making. It was a winter day in the year 1875.

The room was warm and cozy, but outside it was snowing. Thérèse could see the big soft flakes falling against the window where her mother's chair had been drawn to catch the fading light. Thérèse was not yet three years old, but she noticed everything.

She was thinking now that the snowflakes outside looked like the lovely white lace growing under her mother's quick fingers. Later she would learn that her mother was the finest maker of lace in the city of Alençon—and that Alençon, France, was the place where the finest lace in all the world was made.

Crawling closer, she pulled herself up by her mother's skirts and toddled to the window. She put her small nose against the pane, wishing with all her heart that she could catch the snowflakes as they fell. Snow did not come often to Alençon, and when it did, it delighted the children.

"Come back, little one", said her mother. "Come back, and sit here with me. The window is cold. Soon your sisters will return, and Céline will play a fine game with you."

But little Thérèse stayed at the window, and her mother had to rise and carry the small girl back to the cushion at her feet. Thérèse did not mind, for really her favorite place was on the carpet of the cozy sitting room. It was such a lovely carpet with bright red and pink roses woven on it. Now she stretched down a tiny finger and began to trace the outline of one of the big red roses.

"Rose", she said and smiled up at her mother.

"Yes, dearest", replied her mother, bending to stroke the soft golden curls that crowned the small head. "It is a rose. And when summer comes, you will see many like it growing in the garden. Only they will be much lovelier, for they will have been made by the good God himself."

"The good God", repeated Thérèse. But she said it in French, which has a softer sound. "Le bon Dieu", she said.

Her mother was thinking how prettily she smiled and how large and blue were her eyes.

Just then they heard the outer door open, and the happy voices of Thérèse's older sisters filled the hall. They had been out for a romp in the snow. In they came, with faces glowing and eyes dancing. Throwing off their wet coats to dry near the stove, they all began talking at once in their rapid French. Their mother thought they sounded like a flock of young birds, chirping among the apple blossoms that bloomed every springtime against the old stone wall in the garden.

Marie, the oldest, with her big, brown eyes, was as tall as her mother. Because she was almost sixteen and helped greatly with the housekeeping, all the others looked up to her. Little Thérèse, the baby of the family, held up her arms to Marie for a hug and a kiss.

Thérèse had four sisters. After Marie came Pauline, who was fourteen, but *she* was away now at boarding school. Next came Léonie, who was twelve; and then Céline, who was six. With Thérèse, this made five children, four of whom were now gathered about their mother in the warm room.

When Marie had hugged the baby, she reached in her pocket and, to Thérèse's delight, gave her a small piece of chocolate. Then Marie put her arm about her mother's shoulder and bent down to look at the foam of white lace in her lap.

"It's beautiful, Mother!" exclaimed Marie. "The loveliest you ever made! And who is to be lucky enough to own it?"

"The countess de Montfort ordered it for her daughter's wedding dress. But you do not think the thread is too thin, do you, Marie?" she asked worriedly, bending her head to one side as she held the lace up to the light.

"It's perfect", said Marie. "The bride will look like an angel when she wears it."

But as Marie smiled down into her mother's face, she was troubled. It was a lovely face with its straight, slender nose and its large black eyes full of liveliness. But Marie could see now that her mother looked very tired. Once again she was working too hard.

"Why don't you put your work aside and take a little rest before Father comes home?" Marie asked.

"No, no, dear. I am not tired", replied her mother. "And I have only a little more to finish."

"Well then, there's no excuse for me not to be at work", said Marie gaily. "It's almost time for supper, and Louise will be looking for me in the kitchen." And off she flew.

Louise was the maid who took care of the Martin family. Soon Marie was busy helping her fix the evening meal.

Six-year-old Céline had dropped on the floor beside Thérèse, who was laughing happily as her sister pretended she was a little dog on all fours, barking and snapping at the chocolate. But the baby held on to it tightly. Everyone in the room was smiling except Léonie.

"Mother," she was saying, "I want to go away to boarding school, like Pauline."

"So you shall, dear, one day", answered her mother.

"But I want to go *now*", Léonie insisted.

"Why, you are only twelve, Léonie. Pauline, you know, is fourteen."

"But I'm tall for my age, and anyway, I'm tired of it around here."

"Hush, Léonie", said her mother. "You must not let your father hear you say such things. He would be very angry. And he will be home any moment now."

"Father, Father, Father—that's all I hear around this house!" And swooping up her coat, Léonie dashed angrily from the room.

Madame Martin sighed as she laid aside her needle. God had blessed her with five beautiful children.

To be sure, had all her children lived, there would have been nine. Yet God was very good to have spared her the five. But why was it that, of these five, there was only one who gave her any trouble? Léonie, Léonie—she must try to help her overcome angry, unhappy moods. Perhaps the reason she was full of moods and hard to please was that she had been quite ill and had almost died when she was a little girl. Perhaps that was why she was not as happy as the others.

When Louis Martin came home, the onion soup was steaming from the heavy kettle that hung in the great open fireplace. Thérèse heard him at the front door, stamping the snow from his feet. Scrambling from her cushion, she toddled as fast as she could to meet him. Her handsome father swung the child to his shoulder and rubbed his cold cheek against hers. She had her arms tight about his neck, and he went dancing into the sitting room, singing at the same time, "Make way for the Queen! Make way for the Queen!"

That was his special name for Thérèse; and when he was looking for her, he would always ask the others, "Where is my Little Queen?"

As for Thérèse, she was never happier than when in her father's arms.

"Léonie, Léonie," called her mother, "your father is home. It's time to prepare Céline and the baby for supper."

As Louis Martin set Thérèse down and took off his coat, Léonie came slowly down the stairs, thinking, "If I were at boarding school, I would not have this tiresome task to do every evening." But almost at once she was ashamed of herself for this thought. And when she entered she even managed a smile for her father.

"That's my good Léonie", he said as he kissed her.

Then Léonie felt more ashamed of her bad temper and what it had made her say about him.

When they were alone, Madame Martin asked her husband, "Well, Louis dear, did you have any luck?"

"Yes, indeed, my dear Zélie", he exclaimed as he warmed his feet against the stove. "I showed some pieces of your lace to the head of the great firm of Laurent and Company—the largest in Paris. For the next year, he will buy all we can provide."

"Oh, Louis! How wonderful!" exclaimed Madame Martin. "You are truly very clever at business!"

"Nonsense", replied her husband. "It's only because you are such an artist and work so faithfully that the good God has helped us get this order. But now, my dear, you must hire more helpers so that you will be able to make enough lace for our new customer."

The making of Madame Martin's beautiful lace was not simple. Women had to study and practice for years before they could make it. Madame Martin hired other women to stitch the patterns. But, she herself always did the hardest task; she wove the fine strips together.

"Yes, we shall need more help now that we have this large order. We must double the prayers to our Lady and ask her to keep on blessing the work."

"Do not fear. She never fails us", replied her husband. "It was the same when I had my jewelry shop. Ah, how often did our Lady help me!"

"Your charming shop—and the beautiful jewelry you made with your own hands! You are the artist, not I. Oh, Louis, how I hated to see you give up all that!"

"My dear, your lace brings me as much joy as the other work did. Besides, you were killing yourself with overwork. How could anyone take care of a business, a home, and five children besides? It was high time that I gave up the shop and turned to helping such a hard-working wife."

Madame Martin smiled gratefully at her husband. "It still troubles me when I think how much you must miss those beautiful jewels."

"I have six beautiful jewels right here in my own home", said Louis Martin, jumping from his chair and lightly kissing her cheek. "And you are the most beautiful of all!"

"Ah, Louis, I shall become vain", laughed Zélie Martin. "Come, let us go to supper."

Thérèse, holding on to Léonie's hand, now came toddling in with a fresh blue ribbon, the color of her eyes, tied to her tiny curls. Marie was calling them all to supper. When they were seated about the table, her father praised the good onion soup, whose perfume filled the room, and the vegetables Marie and Louise had prepared.

Louise had come to the Martin family from a French farm. She was almost as wide as she was short, but very strong and active. Now, as she served the meal, she joined in suppertime talk as though she were one of the family. She laughed loudly at all Louis Martin's jokes, helped Madame Martin to feed Thérèse, who sat on a high chair at her mother's side, and even gave Céline a quick slap on the hand when she caught her eating too quickly.

When supper was over, Madame Martin herself carried the sleepy Thérèse up to the bedroom she shared with Céline. While all helped to take care of the baby during the day, it was her mother who always put her to bed at night. When she had undressed her, she said, "Now, dear, it is time to kneel down and say your prayers."

The little girl knelt at her mother's knee and folded her small hands. Already she could say the Hail Mary without any help and the Our Father with very little help. Now she turned her head toward the small statue of the Infant Jesus her mother had given her. She had a special prayer for him, which went like this: "Dear little Jesus, bless my mother and father, my sisters, Louise, and little Thérèse. Amen."

It always seemed to her that the Child Jesus was listening and promising her that he would bless everyone. The statue showed him dressed as a little king with a golden crown. It was a copy of the famous statue of the Infant of Prague, her mother explained. Thérèse loved it, for in one hand the Infant Jesus held out a ball. She liked to think that at any moment he would toss it to her, and she could toss it back to him, and they would laugh and play together. When she was a little older she was surprised to learn that what the Child Jesus held was not supposed to be a ball after all—but instead the big round world.

When Madame Martin had tucked Thérèse into bed and kissed her good-night, she blew out the candle and went downstairs to join the others. Céline was also on her way to bed. Then Louis Martin went to the high chest and drew out the checkerboard.

"Who would like a game?" he asked.

But his wife said, "Wait a moment, Louis. First I want to read you the letter that came today from Pauline. You will be happy to learn how well she is doing in the convent at Le Mans!"

"Good!" replied her husband, settling himself in his comfortable chair.

Zélie Martin took the letter from her pocket, handling it as though it were a treasure. Marie hung eagerly over her mother's shoulder to see every line of it for herself. But Léonie started to leave the room. Her father looked at her in surprise.

"Are you not staying to hear your sister's letter?" he asked.

Léonie stopped at the door and hung her head, saying nothing.

"Well?" demanded her father sharply.

She looked up angrily. "No!" she snapped. "I'm going to the kitchen to see Louise."

Her father said sternly, "You will remain here until your mother has read the letter aloud. Sit down!"

Léonie sat. But something deep inside hurt. It was as though some small creature inside her were crying.

Her mother gave her a quick smile. Then she began to read from the letter.

"Dearest Mother and Father, I miss you so much. This year the convent seems lonely without Marie. But I look forward to the spring when I shall be with you all again for the holidays. Then you will see how I have grown and how well I shall be able to help Marie with the housekeeping! Is the baby as pretty as when I last saw her? Mother dear, I hope you are not working too hard. You and Father will be glad to hear that my marks were quite good last month. I came out next to the highest. But I can't wait until I see you again! Will you meet me at the station? Already I can imagine myself on the train. Please give my love to my sisters, and give the baby a special hug from me. I close with love and respect to you, my dear parents. Your Pauline.

"P.S. Aunt Elise sends her love and says to tell you that she is proud of me (for my marks). Pray that I shall do as well this month!"

Aunt Elise was Madame Martin's own sister, who was now a nun in the Visitation Convent at Le Mans, Pauline's school.

"You may go now, Léonie", said her father gravely, and without a word Léonie was off for the kitchen.

As she folded the letter, Zélie Martin smiled happily. "Isn't it wonderful, Louis, that our Pauline is doing so well?"

"Indeed, my dear, very wonderful." Then he added with a twinkle in his eye, "But after all, she should do well. Of all the children, she is the one who is most like her mother!"

"And who am I like?" asked Marie, as she settled herself at the checkerboard with her father.

He looked her up and down teasingly, pretending that he was unable to decide.

"Why, Marie!" exclaimed her mother. "Don't you know? You are just like your father. But you must try to be as good as he is. See how often he goes to church—"

"And fishing", added Marie with a twinkle.

Then they all laughed, and Louis Martin the loudest of all.

"Just for that, I will beat you at checkers, young lady", he said as he began to set out the pieces. His love for fishing was one of the family jokes.

The next day was Sunday, and all, even Thérèse, went to early Mass at the beautiful old Church of Notre Dame. It was amazing how well Thérèse could walk all the way there. She was quick at learning things, thought her father—much quicker than any of the others had been at her age.

On Sundays when the weather was fine, the family would take a walk in the afternoon. These walks always ended again at the church for the evening service of Vespers. Thérèse loved the stained glass windows of Notre Dame. Their lovely colors were soft and glowing, and the light of the setting sun came through them, casting a rainbow of colors upon one side of the white marble altar. She delighted too in the flickering candles and the music that came from the great organ. She would sit very still, very happy, while the service lasted. Now more and more she looked forward to Sundays. . . .

Some months later, in the early spring, the family set out as usual on their Sunday afternoon walk. Thérèse, dancing along at her father's side, was in her best blue dress and blue coat. Madame Martin looked at her daughters with pleasure. She was careful about their clothing, and this afternoon they did indeed look very pretty. It was a lovely sunny day, without a cloud in the sky. But they had not gone very far before a high wind arose. Suddenly dark clouds blew across the face of the sun.

"We shall have rain, I fear", said Louis Martin.

A few moments later it came—at first slowly, and then as the wind rose higher, in a great downpour. Luckily, they were near the home of Louis Martin's mother. They hastened to her door. She was delighted to see them, and she helped the children put their wet coats near the fire to dry. Then she started fixing cups of steaming hot chocolate.

Louis Martin stood at the window, drawing aside the lace curtain to gaze out at the weather. "The rain may end as quickly as it began, and I believe we shall be able to go on to Vespers, after all."

But her mother looked at Thérèse and was uneasy. It would be better not to keep the little one out in such uncertain weather; much better to send her home. One could not tell how the weather would be after Vespers, and she did not wish to risk an illness. A sudden thought struck her that this would be a good way to show Léonie how much the family trusted her and that she was both needed and loved.

"Léonie dear", she said, "I don't want to keep the baby out in this weather. I would like you to take her home now. There is a break in the storm. Perhaps if you hurry you will get home before the next downpour."

A smile lit up Léonie's face. It was an errand of trust. Her mother had not asked Marie, as she usually did, but had asked her! She made up her mind to take every care to fulfill the trust perfectly. "Of course, Mother", she said.

But when Léonie tried to get Thérèse into her coat, the child cried loudly. She seemed to know that she was being taken home and not to her beloved church, Notre Dame. As Léonie tugged her through the wet streets, Thérèse kept hanging back and crying. They arrived at the house breathless, and Léonie was opening the door just as the second downpour burst upon them. The skies were now black; it was as dark as midnight. As Léonie pushed open the door, Louise came running out from the kitchen.

"Thank heaven, someone has come! The kitchen window is stuck fast. I can't close it alone, and the rain is pouring in, all over everything! Come quickly!"

Not stopping to shut the door, Léonie ran to help her. It took quite a while to close the window. When Léonie got back to the hall, Thérèse was gone. She ran into the sitting room, looking for her. It was empty. Then she ran upstairs and looked in all the bedrooms. There was no Thérèse anywhere. She became very frightened. Running down the stairs, she called out to Louise, "The baby! She's gone!"

Then she noticed the open door and went cold with fright. With beating hearts, Louise and Léonie peered out into the darkness and the rain. But there was no sign of Thérèse. Only torrents and torrents of rain—and darkness. Léonie sat down on the stairs and began to cry. "Oh, Louise, they trusted her to me, and I've lost her! We may never find her. Father will be very angry. He will—he may—he will never forgive me!"

2

THE FINE THREAD BREAKS

T HROUGH the dark, wet streets sped Thérèse. The
rain pelted down upon her, dripped into her
eyes from the little blue hat, streamed from the folds
of the pretty blue coat. Her soaking slippers made
her feet heavy, but she hurried all the faster. She
must see the candles and hear the beautiful music.

She didn't feel that she was being naughty, for her

beautiful stone church, Notre Dame, was calling her with a whisper she could not resist. Despite the darkness, she found her way. Her small feet took her surely down the streets and around the turns where she had so often walked with her family.

It was Louise who found her. She had lost no time in going after Thérèse. Throwing a coat over her broad shoulders, she had been out the door in a flash —leaving Léonie helpless and weeping upon the stairs.

Later Louise, standing in the middle of the sitting room, with her hands on her hips, told the exciting story to the family.

"I guessed that the little one would make straight for the church. So off I went after her. Since Noah there was never such a flood! I feared the baby would be drowned before I could find her. In the darkness she could so easily have stumbled into the river.

"But at last I spied her, almost at the door of the church. I swooped down upon her—and caught her up in my arms. Then you have never heard such a screaming and crying as I turned back toward home. She beat at my face with her little fists, saying she *would* go to church. She kicked and she clawed, but I held on fast. And now there she lies upstairs, safe and asleep, after a warm bath and some good hot soup inside her!"

Zélie and Louis Martin were very grateful to Louise. But Léonie sat trembling, head down and with red eyes, in a corner. Her father came over to her, lifted her chin, and looked into her face.

"There, there, Léonie; do not cry. The good God has saved your little sister. And you, my dear, have been taught a lesson."

Léonie's face showed her gratitude. Her mother followed her upstairs, turned down her bed, and got out her nightgown, talking cheerfully all the time. "You did very well, dear," she said, "for while it was careless not to close the door, still you were trying to help someone who was in need—someone who had called to you for help. Sometimes in life, it happens that way. Sometimes there are two who need us at the same moment, and it is not always easy to know which one must come first. But if we do our best, God understands, even if we make mistakes."

As Léonie drifted off to sleep, she thought she had the best parents in all the world. And she made up her mind never to give them any trouble again.

Marie was up early the next morning, helping Louise with the baking. They were fixing extra little cakes for Pauline's homecoming. She was arriving the following afternoon. Marie could hardly wait. There was so much she wanted to hear about the convent where she herself had been a student last year, so much about the girls and the nuns and Pauline's courses. There was less than two years' difference between Marie and Pauline, and they had always been very close.

On this early morning, six-year-old Céline, who slept in the room with Thérèse, was awakened by hearing her big sister go softly down the stairs. Céline wondered what on earth Marie was doing so early in the morning. Perhaps there was some fun in all this. Laughter was bubbling up inside Céline. She always awakened that way—she could not help it. And now, with the birds singing in the trees outside, she felt she could not bear staying in bed another moment. Sliding from under the covers and without even stopping for slippers, she followed Marie, arriving in the kitchen clad only in her white nightgown.

Louise had already started a good fire, and Marie was opening the big flour bin. She was scooping some flour into a bowl when suddenly they both caught sight of Céline. She was standing on one foot in the doorway, eyeing them mischievously.

"Céline! Go straight back to bed", ordered Marie.

But as Marie put the bowl of flour down on the table, Céline only came farther into the kitchen.

"Cakes! We're going to have cakes!" Céline cried, dancing around the plump Louise and pulling at her apron strings. Louise reached out to box her on the ear, but Céline was too quick for her and scampered off toward the door. Thinking that she was gone, the two in the kitchen set about their work. But Céline was peeping at them from the doorway, and when both had their backs turned, she crept swiftly back and made for the flour bin.

When Marie turned suddenly, a strange sight met her eyes. There stood Céline in her white night-gown, with her face and neck, her hands and feet, completely covered with flour. Except for her dancing brown eyes, from top to toe she was stark white. Even her hair was powdered. Marie and Louise stared at her, too startled to move.

"I'm a ghost!" cried Céline. "Boo! Boo!" And she waved her white arms at them.

"My good flour", gasped Louise and made for her. But Céline dodged and in a flash was out the door and speeding up the stairs with her head down and flapping her white hands.

"I'm a ghost! I'm a ghost!" she kept crying. But suddenly, when she had almost reached the top step, her outstretched head hit something soft but immovable. Terrified, she looked up into her father's startled face. Her head had hit him in the middle, and his dark suit was now covered with flour. She expected a storm of anger. But as she stood there trembling, Louis Martin just sat down on the stairs and shook with laughter.

"Oh, Father! I didn't mean—oh, don't tell Mother!"

"Very well, young lady. But you had better see to it that all that flour on the stairs is cleaned up before your mother returns from early Mass! And clean yourself too before the baby sees you. We don't want her frightened by a ghost."

The next afternoon, the family stood on the platform of the Alençon station, waiting for the train from Le Mans that was bringing Pauline. Although she tried to be calm, Madame Martin's heart was fluttering like a hummingbird. She always felt like this when Pauline came home. The child had been away from her too long. Truly, it had been hard to part with her—yet with Pauline's good mind it was important that she should have more schooling. And this she could best receive at the convent in Le Mans.

Marie stood by her mother, while Léonie held Céline firmly by the hand. Louis Martin was holding Thérèse in his arms to keep her from running out on the tracks. When the train came around a bend and began puffing its way into the station, Thérèse tried to wriggle from her father's arms. She liked the great cloud of gray smoke that poured from the train and drifted into the sky, but the noisy "chug-chug" that went with it frightened her.

"There, there, Little Queen, you are quite safe", said her father, and Thérèse settled back quietly.

When Pauline stepped from the train and ran to them with open arms, her father thought how tall she had grown. She was even more like her mother than when she had left home. She had the same lively black eyes, the same fine nose and sweet, firm mouth. They were all hugging each other and talking at once. Marie took the baby from her father so that he could carry Pauline's bag. Once they were out of the station, Marie set her down, and Thérèse ran happily along beside her.

They had cakes after supper that evening, and then there was much laughter in the sitting room as Pauline told them funny things that had happened at the convent. Louis Martin sang some of the old French songs. Thérèse was allowed to stay up half an hour later than usual. She sat quite still on her father's lap, delighting in his voice. She was happy that her pretty sister Pauline had come home. Life was wonderful.

Now that Pauline was home, Léonie had to give up the bed in which she had been sleeping, so that Marie and Pauline could be together. A bed had been made up for Léonie on the third floor. She seemed not to mind this, yet she thought to herself, "I am just the odd child. I never *will* be closest to anyone. Everyone in this family is paired off—except me. Mother and Father are a pair; Marie and Pauline are a pair; Céline and Thérèse are a pair. But I'm all by myself—except for Louise."

She sighed as she thought how different it all would have been, had little Hélène lived. Less than two years younger than Léonie, she had died when she was five. But before that, they had enjoyed wonderful times together. When Léonie finally fell asleep, her pillow was wet with tears.

Although Marie and Pauline were a pair, yet Pauline was as much with Thérèse during the days that followed as she was with her older sister. The baby delighted her. She was so lively and quick to understand. In the garden, their father had put up a swing for Thérèse, hanging it from a big tree. Pauline was her faithful playmate there, standing behind her and pushing the wooden seat so that Thérèse, singing and laughing, could soar higher and higher.

Although Pauline had tied Thérèse to the swing, it made Madame Martin very nervous to watch her youngest child flying so high through the air. Secretly she wished that Thérèse would be content to play with dolls. They were so much safer! But Thérèse did not care very much for dolls. The playthings she liked best were her top and her little wooden horn.

And her favorite pets were her chicks. There was a chickenhouse in the garden, and this spring her father had given her some tiny yellow chicks all for her own. Céline and she had great fun, trying to catch the lively little things and stroke their feathers.

Her father, with his fine jeweler's fingers, was very good at making toys, and these she liked best of all. For her he made little figures out of wood and put a piece of heavy lead in their feet. Thérèse would knock them over, but at once they would bob up again—all by themselves.

As Thérèse wondered at this, her father would say, "You must learn to be like them. Whenever you fall down, or things go wrong, you must bob right up again, smiling."

This Thérèse tried very hard to do. The spring and summer passed happily, and in the fall, Pauline started back to school. Léonie went to classes in town, and Marie taught Céline at home. Marie would let Thérèse sit with them if she promised to be quiet. Soon Thérèse was learning almost as quickly as Céline.

When the warm weather came again and the first rosebuds appeared in the garden, her mother took Thérèse by the hand and showed them to her. Not long after, Thérèse ran in great excitement to her mother, "Come, look!" she cried. "See the beautiful red rose the good God made last night in our garden!"

Another summer was smiling on Alençon, and Pauline was home again. One June morning when the girls were outdoors, their father was working at his desk in the sitting room. The desk was covered with books and papers, for he was going over the accounts of the lace business. Zélie Martin, as usual, was in her chair near the window, busy with her needle.

"We have made quite a bit of money this month", said her husband, looking up from his books.

"That's because you worked so hard in Paris last week", Zélie Martin replied. "But I fear you pushed yourself too hard. You came home looking very tired."

"Not at all", denied her husband, going back to his accounts.

"Are the bills very heavy?" asked his wife.

"Well, they are rather high", he sighed. "We paid the workers more than usual this month. And I see that the cost of thread has gone up."

"Yes", she agreed. "The price of the fine thread is very high."

"Well, in spite of the bills and high costs, we are still putting money aside", said Louis Martin. "If all goes well, soon we shall be able to take things more easily."

"Oh, Louis, I look forward to the time when we can have some of those wonderful trips you have always wanted."

"We shall go first to Italy", said Louis Martin with a happy smile in his eyes. "And then perhaps on to the Holy Land."

"Why don't you take a little trip this afternoon— to the Pavilion, perhaps?" asked his wife. "You do look tired, Louis, and the fresh air—"

"If you will come with me!" he interrupted.

"No, dear, I can't", she sighed. "The workers are coming this afternoon. But the girls would love to go with you."

"I won't go unless you promise to take a few days of rest soon", said Louis Martin. "You are the one who has been working too hard."

"Well, perhaps next week I shall go to Lisieux for

a few days", she replied. "My brother has written me to come, and I could take Céline and Thérèse with me."

"Splendid!" cried her husband. "That's just what you need."

At Lisieux, a few miles north of Alençon, lived Zélie Martin's only brother, Isidore Guérin, and his charming wife. Madame Martin was very fond of both of them, and they had two little girls who were much loved by the Martin children. The young cousins were named Jeanne and Marie. Jeanne was about Céline's age, and Marie was three years older than Thérèse.

The Guérin family often visited the Martins, and then there would be parties and trips, and everyone had a happy time. Zélie Martin's brother was a successful chemist in Lisieux. His wife had the same name as Céline, and the Martin girls called her Aunt Céline. It was odd too that each family had a daughter named Marie. When one Marie was called, and the *other* Marie ran, it led to many jokes and much laughter.

"What a pity", they all often said to each other, "that we don't live in the same city! Then we could see each other every day."

Secretly that was just what Madame Martin had always wished—that her daughters might grow up near their cousins and their aunt and uncle.

On this June morning as she sat with her husband,

planning her trip to Lisieux, the hours passed quickly, and soon it was time for the midday meal. When they were all seated at the table, Louis Martin asked: "Who would like to join me this afternoon for a walk to the Pavilion?"

Each of the five girls cried at once, "I would!"

"Not *all* of you?" asked their father in mock alarm.

"Please, please, Father!" they begged.

"Very well, then. But I shall look like a school teacher with his class, walking through the streets with five lively girls at my heels."

The Martin girls loved the Pavilion. It belonged to their father, and they took great pride in it. It was really a tiny private home in a quiet part of Alençon. It was hidden from the street by a high stone wall with a locked gate. A beautiful garden circled the house, which was built almost like a tower. One could enter it only by climbing an outside staircase. But it was really a small house even for one or two people, so, of course, the family could not live there. Long before he had been married, Louis Martin had bought it as a place where he could read and study and be alone. He still kept many of his books there and all his treasured fishing tackle.

As the girls prepared for their little trip, they were in a flutter of excitement. Céline, who could not find her hat, had run to her mother's closet and taken down her best bonnet. With that on her head, she pranced into the upstairs hall, holding her skirts high and acting as if she were a great lady. Everyone laughed, but Marie snatched the bonnet from her head and put it carefully back where it belonged. She found Céline's hat under the bed where it had rolled. Soon they all came down the stairs to join their father, who was waiting in the hall. Last of all, and slowly, came Léonie.

Seeing that she wore no hat, her father asked in surprise, "You're not coming with us, Léonie?"

She hung her head. "I've changed my mind, Father. I would rather stay here. Louise said that if I would sit with her in the kitchen, she would teach me how to knit."

Madame Martin, who was writing a letter in the sitting room, heard Léonie through the open door. She laid down her pen and sighed. This strange child—if only she would be like the others! Well, they must pray more for Léonie. As their father held the door open, the others went out gaily, for long ago they had learned not to mind Léonie's moods. Thérèse and her father walked along, hand in hand.

When they reached the Pavilion and their father unlocked the high gate, Thérèse was the first to scramble up the steps. She ran straight for the garden where the rosebushes were in bloom. There were more roses here than at home, for the garden was larger. In the Pavilion gardens were pink and yellow roses. But best of all, Thérèse loved the great, dark red ones that hung their velvety heads on a level with her own.

In the center of the garden was a little block of stone. Her father pointed to it now and said, "Right there is where the statue of our Lady used to stand!"

Marie said, "It must have looked beautiful there, with the roses all about it—more beautiful than it looks now at home. Perhaps our Lady would like it better if we brought her statue back to the Pavilion."

But Pauline said, "Oh, no! We would miss it so much if it were taken from our room."

And their father said, "When you two oldest girls were born, your mother insisted that the statue should always be in your room."

At home every evening before supper, Pauline would take Thérèse to the little altar on which the statue stood and would teach her to say prayers to our Lady. All the Martin girls loved the statue because it showed our Lady smiling. There were stars about her head, and she stretched out her hands to bless them as she smiled. Their father had told them that it was a copy of a very famous statue called "Our Lady of the Smile". More than a hundred years ago, it had been made in silver for a French monastery. Everyone liked it so well that many copies of it had since been made.

Now, in the garden of the Pavilion, Thérèse reached up and gently touched one of the big red roses. "Take home to our Lady?" she asked her father.

"Yes, you may have some roses to take home to our Lady's altar", he said. "But we shall not cut them until we are ready to leave."

Céline had run up the outside staircase of the house and was begging her father to unlock the door.

"Now, don't touch the fishing rods", he told them all, as he turned the key.

Pauline went over at once to the books that lined the shelves around the big fireplace.

Marie entered the tiny kitchen. "I would love to keep house here", she said. "Did you really cook meals here, Father?"

"Indeed yes," he replied, "and very good they were."

Céline said teasingly, "Lucky for us that Father does not cook now!"

"Ho, ho", said her father. "So you think I can't cook? Let me tell you, young lady, that every true Frenchman knows how to cook from the day he is born."

Céline ran over to the little staircase and scrambled up it like a monkey. She called down from the second floor. "Oh, Father! May I dress up in this lovely bedspread?"

"Yes, yes," he replied, "as long as you stay away from me and the fishing tackle."

He had gone over to his favorite corner where stood all his rods and was now busy sorting out his hooks and lines. Thérèse sat quietly at his feet, watching him. Finally, she said gravely, "If you were to take me fishing with you, I would catch a big, fat fish, and we could eat it for supper."

"Why, that's a fine idea, Thérèse", he said, patting his little daughter on the head.

When they returned home, Thérèse was carrying a bunch of red roses. At once, she ran upstairs to place them on our Lady's altar. But the very small roses she took into her own room and put them at the feet of the Infant Jesus, whose little statue stood at the head of her bed.

"Here are some flowers for you. But I do wish you would play a little with me and the ball", she whispered.

When Louis Martin entered the sitting room, his wife was just saying good-night to her workers, with whom she had been sewing all afternoon. She looked very pale and tired.

"My dear Zélie," he said when the helpers had gone, "you must *not* work so hard."

"I'm not really tired, Louis", she replied. "And just think—in a few days I shall be on my way to Lisieux for a lovely little holiday!"

But the next day, Zélie Martin was not able to leave her bed. At first they thought that she was merely tired. But soon they knew that she was very ill. The next day, the doctor was called. But nothing he could do seemed to help her. As the days passed, she only grew worse. In great worry, Louis Martin wrote to the Guérin family in Lisieux, saying that his wife was too ill now to visit them. The unhappy girls tiptoed quietly about the house, trying to think of things they could do for their mother. Every day they went to early Mass with their father to pray that she would get better quickly.

Each morning, Thérèse brought her mother some flowers from the garden. It made her feel better to see her mother smile at her.

Léonie spent long hours alone in the attic. She could cry there, and no one could see her. If only Mother would get better! But every day she grew worse. And Léonie felt there was something she must tell her mother. One day she crept down the stairs from the attic and washed the tears from her face. Then, with a brave smile, she went into her mother's room. "I want to tell you something", she said.

"Yes, dear", whispered her mother, reaching up for Léonie's hand.

"I have not been a very good girl around this house", Léonie started bravely. "But now I promise you that after this, I shall be better. I shall try to be as you have always wanted me to be."

Zélie Martin searched her daughter's face and saw there for the first time a new look of resolution. Then over her own face there spread a beautiful smile. She sank back on the pillows with a sigh of happiness.

"Thank you, dearest. You know, Léonie, I have always wanted all my girls to become real saints. So when the good God carries me to heaven, do not forget that I shall be praying for all of you, and especially for my dear Léonie."

Even though there were tears running down her cheeks, Léonie was happier than she had ever been before. She felt as though a great stone had been lifted from her heart.

The next morning, Aunt Céline and Uncle Isidore arrived from Lisieux. Aunt Céline was so pretty and so kind, they all thought. It helped to have her there.

Then came a day that Thérèse would never forget. She was awakened early by her father, who was leaning over her bed. He picked her up in his arms and said gently, "Come and kiss your poor little mother for the last time."

Then he called Céline. She followed them as he carried Thérèse into their mother's room. Marie, Pauline, and Léonie were already there.

As Thérèse leaned down from her father's arms and kissed her mother's cheek, she thought, "How beautiful mother looks! She looks just like her own lace." And indeed, Zélie Martin's face with its happy smile looked as fine and as lovely and as white as the lace she made.

"Her soul has flown into the arms of the good God", explained their father.

Then Aunt Céline took Thérèse into her arms, and little Thérèse clung to her.

3

THE NEW GARDEN

A LTHOUGH it was a cold November day, the door
of the house in Lisieux stood wide open. Marie,
shivering in spite of her warm shawl, was half out of
the door as she directed the men who came lumber-
ing up the garden steps and across the front lawn.
They carried pieces of furniture on their backs, for
the Martin family had moved from Alençon to

Lisieux. Marie looked at every piece carefully to make sure that there had been no damage and that everything was there.

Aunt Céline, wrapped in furs, stood in the hall of the pretty country house with Pauline and Léonie at her elbow, ready to run anywhere at her bidding. But it was Léonie who with a smile insisted on doing the most unpleasant jobs. How helpful she is, thought her aunt, and how much she has changed in these past weeks from the Léonie we all used to know.

On this busy morning, there was work for everyone—everyone, that is, but Céline and Thérèse, who now were out exploring the large garden behind the house. It was surrounded by thick shrubbery and bushes, and there were lovely woodlands just beyond. What a heavenly place to play! It was much larger than their garden at Alençon had been.

"Look!" called Thérèse. "There's a special place just for the rose bushes!"

As they came upon one beautiful spot after another, they gasped with pleasure. So many things to explore were here. Suddenly they found a hidden woodshed.

"For our little chicks", Thérèse pointed out.

Céline then discovered an old, filled-in well in the garden. A little roof made of logs stood on poles above the well.

Scampering under the roof, Céline said, "We can

pretend that this is our own house. Perhaps Marie will let us have parties out here."

"Come and look", called Thérèse, who had run again toward the front of the house. "Now the men are carrying our Lady up the steps!"

Although the statue was well wrapped, Thérèse knew from its shape that it was Our Lady of the Smile. Céline ran to join her, and together they heard their aunt's voice.

"That goes in the hall", she was saying to the men.

"Oh no", called Marie from the doorway. "It goes upstairs in the large bedroom next to Father's. Mother always wanted Pauline and me to have Our Lady of the Smile in our room."

"I don't think it's fair", whispered Céline to Thérèse. "Just because they're the oldest, they have our Lady. Why can't we ever have the statue in *our* room?"

Thérèse opened her blue eyes very wide. "But we have the Infant Jesus", she reminded her sister. "And when the roses come, we can make a lovely altar for him."

Soon Victoire, the new maid whom Aunt Céline had found for them, came to get them. Already the two youngest girls loved her.

"Come," said Victoire, "the men have finished, and your uncle's carriage is here to take us all back to his house for the night. But tomorrow, we shall be sleeping here."

All during the drive back to the Guérin house, the girls talked excitedly about their new home. Their uncle seemed greatly pleased that they liked it so much.

"It was hard to find just what your father wanted", he explained to Marie. "He wrote that he needed a house in the country with plenty of grounds for the children, and yet one near the city too, and above all, near a church!"

"That was like Father", said Marie. "But how clever you were to find just the right thing for him! He will be delighted. I can't wait to have him see it."

Louis Martin had remained in Alençon to sell the old house and to close out the Martin lace business. Crushed by the death of his wife, he had no heart to go on with the business that would always remind him of her. So he had asked his brother-in-law to find a house for him in Lisieux.

When it had been found, Louis Martin sent his girls ahead, under the care of seventeen-year-old Marie. Their aunt and uncle had met them at the station and had taken them into their own home until the new house could be fixed.

After their mother's death, it had been very sad there in the old house in Alençon. They were glad when their father told them that they were to make a new home in Lisieux. Every corner of the old house reminded them of their mother. The adventure of moving to a new city and of making a new home there for their father had helped them to forget some of their sadness.

As for Thérèse, she could not help but think how happy her dear mother must be up there in heaven with the good God. Some day they would all be together again. Until then, she must try to remember every little thing her mother had taught her.

On this November evening, when the carriage drew up before the Guérins' home, the girls tumbled out to be greeted merrily at the door by their cousins, Jeanne and Marie. Jeanne, only a year older than Céline, took her off to show her the new doll's dress she had just made. Marie, three years older than Thérèse, looked upon her young cousin as her own special charge.

"Come", she said, taking her by the hand. "Marcelline has made some fresh cookies, and she said we could each have one." And off they went to the kitchen.

The next day the Guérin family and the two maids, Victoire and Marcelline, helped the Martins settle their new home. By evening, much of it was in order, and Aunt Céline felt well pleased as she kissed the girls good-night and drove off with her own family.

"Now, all is ready for Louis", she said to her husband. "I only hope he will be pleased. For girls who are still so young, Marie and Pauline are fine housekeepers. Your sister trained them well. With Victoire, who seems to be a good maid, they should manage very well for poor Louis."

Then she sighed, for she knew, as did her husband, that nothing ever again would be very happy for Louis Martin.

All during the long day that her father was expected, Thérèse stayed near the front gate of their new home. When at last she heard the carriage on the road below, she ran to meet him with open arms. He caught her up as he had always done and swung her to his shoulder.

"The Little Queen herself!" he cried. "And how does she like her new palace?"

Once inside the house, there was much excitement as he was led to see one marvel after another. Everything about the new home pleased him, and he especially liked the large windows that looked out on the garden. Marie led him over to the handsome clock on the mantelpiece.

"It is one of your own clocks that you made!" she exclaimed.

"Why, so it is", said her father, much pleased that she had thought to place it there. And then to tease her, he added, "I'm surprised that you remembered to pack it."

"Would we forget, when everyone has always said that you were the best clock-maker in all Alençon?" asked Pauline.

At last they led him up to his own room in the front of the house. Here they had put everything for his comfort. He sank down in his own easy chair and looked at his big desk and the fine new curtains.

"Why," he said, "you have made this room so comfortable that I shall be spending all my time here." Then he put his arm about Thérèse, and asked, "What, then, will become of all our fishing trips, Little Queen?"

"Oh, when summer is here, we shall go fishing every day". she told him.

Later that evening, when they were gathered in the warm sitting room, Céline and Thérèse sat down together on a little bench near the fireplace.

Their father came over to them and said, "Now that your dear mother is with the good God, your big sisters shall be second mothers to you. We shall call them little mothers. So now each of you should choose her own little mother and promise to obey her always."

Céline was off the bench in a flash and had thrown her arms about Marie. "I choose Marie for my little mother!" she cried.

Thérèse hesitated only for a moment. She, too, had wanted to choose Marie, for, after all, Marie was the oldest of the family. But she had caught a glimpse of Pauline's face, and suddenly she knew that she must not hurt Pauline's feelings. So at once she flew over and, hugging Pauline, asked, "Please, Pauline, will you be my little mother?"

Pauline beamed and gave her a big hug. "Of course, Thérèse. But you must promise to be a very good girl."

"I will", said Thérèse and nodded her curly head firmly.

All this time Léonie sat quietly, with a sad little smile on her face. Louis Martin laid a hand on her shoulder.

"It is Léonie who is going to look after me", he said. "After all, I have to have someone too—to see to my desk and my clothing and all my things when I am away."

Léonie's face lit up with a big smile. "Oh, I shall be glad to, Father!"

"You shall have complete charge," he said, "even of my letters when I am not here."

So Léonie ended with what each of Louis Martin's daughters thought was the greatest honor of all.

When the two little ones had been put to bed, their father said to the others, "We have not said good-bye to Alençon completely, you know. I shall still go there often to see your grandmother. For that reason, while I have sold the old house, we still own our Pavilion."

Marie clapped her hands, while the others smiled delightedly.

"And sometimes," their father went on, "one or

two of you may come with me on my visits, to see your old friends."

The girls were delighted with this idea. Life was beginning well in the new home. It was to be a busy home, with each of the three oldest daughters having special duties. And that night, the silent prayers of each were alike: "Dear God, please help me to do my task well." Marie was thinking of her charge, Céline; Pauline was thinking of Thérèse; and Léonie, of their father.

At some distance from the Martins' new home lay the convent of the Benedictine nuns, where Jeanne and Marie Guérin went to school. When the new term opened, one of Léonie's dearest wishes came true. Since she was now almost fifteen, her father entered her there as a student in the boarding school. It was decided too that Céline, who would soon be nine, should go to day school with her cousins, Jeanne and Marie.

When Céline started school, Thérèse for the first time in her life was left without a playmate. Of course, every day she was busy for a few hours with the lessons Marie taught her. And every night her little mother Pauline read aloud to her. Sometimes she read from the holy Gospels and sometimes from the *Lives of the Saints*. Thérèse was happy, listening to these stories and also to tales of the glory of France. She loved hearing about Joan of Arc, who led the armies of France to victory.

"When I grow up, I am going to be a great soldier like Joan of Arc, and I will save France", she told Pauline.

But in the hours when she was free to run in the garden, she was lonely without Céline. One night, just before going to sleep, she whispered to the statue of the Infant Jesus, "If you would only bring your ball and play with me in the garden, I would not miss Céline so much."

The next day, as she was gathering little stones in the garden to make a shrine beside the bushes, she suddenly felt she was not alone. She could see no one, but she felt very happy.

"Is that you, Little Jesus, and have you brought your ball?"

She stopped her work to listen for the answer, but she heard only the wind sighing softly through the trees. But in her heart she felt that he was there. So now she said to him, "It is not very polite of me to ask you to bring your ball. Since you are God, I should bring a ball to you. Could I myself be your little ball? Then you could toss me wherever you pleased. I would not mind, even if you went off and forgot about me. I would just wait until you had come to find me again. Please, dear Jesus, make me into your own little ball, so that sometimes I may rest in your hands."

And now, every night before falling asleep, she said the same prayer. In the hours when she was alone, she began to think more about the things her mother had taught her. She would reach into her pocket for the string of beads her mother had made for her.

"See, Thérèse", her mother had said. "With these beads you can count the things you do to please the Infant Jesus. Every time during the day when you give up something you want in order to please him, you must push a bead over this knot on the string. Then, at the end of the day, you can count the beads that show how many things you did for him. The more there are, the better he will be pleased."

Thérèse was always watching for the chance to do something or to give up something for the Infant Jesus. She began with little things. When Victoire spoke crossly to her about leaving the kitchen door open—and it had really been the grocer's boy who had done it—Thérèse was silent and took the scolding. She knew that she did not deserve the scolding, and it was very hard not to defend herself, but this was her way of doing something for the Infant Jesus.

There were many days when Thérèse did not feel that the Infant Jesus had come to play with her in the garden, and without Céline, the garden was very lonely. Of course, there was always the swing that her father had hung behind the woodshed. And in the woodshed itself was a delightful family of white rabbits he had given her.

But one day Thérèse said to him, "The rabbits seem lonely, and I think they would like to have a little dog to play with them."

"Ho, ho", said her father. "So it's only the *rabbits* who are lonely? Well, we can't have that."

The next day, when Thérèse had finished her lessons, she ran into the garden. A lovely white spaniel came romping to meet her. In delight, she dropped on her knees to pet him. He jumped up and licked her face and then rolled over, laughing, at her feet. This was how the two, who were to become such great friends, first met.

Her father, who was watching, said, "Thérèse, this is Tom. And Tom, this is Thérèse."

Tom seemed to understand perfectly, for he stood close to her and looked up at her, wagging his tail so fast that Thérèse was almost afraid it would come off.

When the fine weather came, Thérèse and Tom went fishing with Louis Martin. They had a hard time at first keeping Tom from jumping into the stream and frightening the fish. But he soon learned to play with Thérèse in the fields, while her father sat on the bank with his long fishing rod and pulled out the trout.

On Sundays, and indeed on most weekdays, the whole family went to Mass at the Church of Saint Pierre. Every Sunday evening Aunt Céline invited one of the girls and their father for supper. The girls took turns, and Thérèse was very happy when her turn came, for it gave her a chance to see Jeanne and Marie. Léonie and Céline saw them every day at school.

Three happy years passed in this way. Thérèse was eight years old when Léonie finished school and came home to stay.

"Now it is *your* turn to go to the convent, Little Queen", said her father. "So when the new term begins, you will start off every morning with Céline."

Thérèse and Céline were delighted with this idea. On the first day of school, they set out with light hearts. But as soon as they reached the convent, Thérèse was left in one room while Céline went to another, for Céline belonged in a higher grade. Thérèse was frightened when the reverend mother questioned her. In answer to the questions, she tried hard to remember all that Marie had taught her. But she felt very stupid indeed.

Then the reverend mother said, "You have been well prepared at home—in fact, so well that I shall place you in a class of girls older than yourself."

This frightened Thérèse even more. One of the nuns took her to a classroom full of older girls, who stared at her and made her feel very uncomfortable. Everything seemed strange and new. As the days passed, she felt very unhappy. She kept wishing that she were at home with Pauline reading to her about the great deeds of Joan of Arc and with Tom waiting out in the garden for a good romp. She learned her lessons quickly, but she felt very shy with the older girls and found nothing to say to them. She was the youngest in the class. And apart from Céline, her only playmate during recess was her cousin Marie.

The oldest girl in the class was so unkind to Thérèse that Thérèse wanted to run whenever she saw her coming. The girl's name was Francine, and she was fourteen years old. From the start, she had been jealous of Thérèse—a fact Thérèse never guessed. But fourteen-year-old Francine did not like it that Thérèse, who was only eight, consistently received the highest marks. So she was always looking for a way to tease her.

Thérèse longed to tell her father that she was unhappy and to ask him to take her out of school. But she said to herself, "I promised the Infant Jesus I would not complain." And she made up her mind to try her best to like school. As long as she could talk things over at the day's end with her little mother Pauline, she could bear her troubles at school. Pauline seemed to understand everything.

One afternoon, when school was over and all the children were leaving, Louis Martin stood at the convent gate, waiting for Thérèse and Céline. When he was not away on business, he always called for them. And as they ran to meet him on this day, Francine happened to be right behind them. As their father held out his arms to his daughters, he asked

Thérèse, "And how did my Little Queen do in school today?"

The next afternoon at recess, while Thérèse was quietly playing with Marie, Francine stood laughing and whispering with a group of older girls. Suddenly they walked over toward the two cousins.

Francine stepped up to Thérèse and bowed low before her. Then she asked teasingly, "Your Highness, Little Queen, may we use the playground?"

Then the other big girls also bowed low and giggled as they cried, "The Little Queen! The Little Queen!"

Thérèse blushed up to the roots of her hair. She wanted to run, but they had circled her. If only the ground would open and swallow her! But there was no escape. She stood there, shaking and trying to keep back the tears.

Eleven-year-old Marie was furious. She stepped in front of Thérèse and exclaimed, "Yes, my cousin *is* a Little Queen! That is how we all think of her. Are any of *you* called queens in your own families?"

And turning her back on them, she took Thérèse by the arm and led her away. Thérèse wanted to hide from them forever. All that day her heart felt as though it were breaking.

Francine did not love her. None of those older girls loved her. They hated her. She did not understand. At home, everyone had always loved her.

4

BEHIND THE HIGH HEDGE

Pauline, as usual, had been wonderful. At the end of that terrible day, Louis Martin had not called at the convent for Céline and Thérèse, for he had left Lisieux on a business trip that very afternoon. So they had walked home with their cousins, Jeanne and Marie.

Later that evening, when Thérèse cried out her

story on Pauline's shoulder, Pauline stroked her golden hair and spoke to her quietly. "Now you see, dear, that all is not love in the world, as it should be. It is sad, because God wants his children to love him and to love one another. But evil enters into our weak hearts and causes unhappiness by killing love."

"Francine does not love me", sobbed Thérèse.

"No, she does not love you", agreed Pauline. "But that is because evil has entered into the poor child's heart. And now she is helpless. It made her unkind to you this afternoon. But deep down inside her, she did not wish to hurt you. Right now, she is probably sorry and unhappy. For she is a child of God, and she was meant to love him and all his other children. So we must forgive Francine—"

"Oh, I do, I do!" interrupted Thérèse.

"And we must pray a great deal for her, asking that God's grace will drive the evil from her heart and that she will be happy again as she was meant to be. For right now, I am sure that she is a very unhappy girl—far more unhappy than you are."

"Poor Francine", said Thérèse, sitting up and wiping her eyes. After a little while, she added, "Let us not tell Father anything about it. It would only make him unhappy that his words were overheard and were used to hurt me."

"That is wise", agreed Pauline. "We shall say nothing to him about it. And because your decision will please the Infant Jesus, I think you may slip another bead along your string."

Thérèse hugged her and went off to bed with a great load lifted from her heart. She fell asleep, praying for poor Francine.

There was another convent in Lisieux besides the one where the girls went to school. It was quite a different sort of convent. In their long walks together, Thérèse and her father had often passed it. It was hidden from the street by a wall and a high hedge. But when one came to the gate, one could peep through and see the front of the tall, white building inside. High above the entrance, there was a marble statue of our Lady, and underneath the statue were these words: *Our Lady of Mount Carmel, pray for us.*

The first time that Thérèse and her father had passed the gate, he had told her, "Beyond this gate live the holiest women in Lisieux. They spend their lives praying for all poor sinners."

"May we go in and see them?" asked Thérèse.

"Oh, no," replied her father, "for they live apart from the world. They have learned that the more removed they are from people, the closer they can come to the good God."

Thérèse was silent, as she thought about this.

"You don't understand, Little Queen?" asked her father.

She nodded her head and said, "Oh, yes, I *do* understand!"

For she knew that she herself had come closer to the Infant Jesus during the long days she had spent in the garden alone, when Céline had gone off to school for the first time. That was when she felt that he had really come to be her dearest friend. That was when she felt that she was learning how to be used as his little ball.

Sometimes in the summer, after a happy afternoon of fishing, Thérèse, her father, and Tom would stop a moment at the door of the convent to leave a basket of fish for the nuns.

"These nuns are very poor", Thérèse's father explained to her. "They have given up everything to come closer to the good God. They allow themselves very little to eat and are often hungry. Let us try not to forget them. We should give them all we can spare."

"Do they teach school like our Benedictine nuns?" asked Thérèse.

"Oh, no", answered her father. "They spend most of their time in prayer, although they also work hard at their duties in the convent. They are called Carmelite nuns, and their house is known as the Carmel of Lisieux."

Often the Martin girls would join in fixing a basket of food for the nuns in the convent behind the high hedge. Always it would contain freshly baked bread and sometimes a few jars of jelly. Pauline would pack the basket carefully and carry it to the

Carmel. The girls would not let Victoire help them at all with these baskets.

Victoire had a romance that greatly interested the whole family. Every Sunday afternoon a young man came to call upon her. His name was Léon, and he would appear wearing a stiff hat and a high collar, holding a stiff little bunch of flowers for Victoire. Sometimes they would go for a walk, and sometimes they would sit in the garden—that is, if Céline were not around. For, as Victoire explained to Léon, "You never can tell what *that* young mischief may be up to." Léon was a clerk in a store in Lisieux.

"You must not bother Victoire when Léon comes to see her", said Marie to the younger girls. "You should keep out of the way."

One warm Saturday in the summer of 1882, Céline and Thérèse had run out to the garden right after lunch. They had a romp with Tom, and then Thérèse suggested that they should trim the grass around the rose garden, which was now in full bloom. This sounded too tame for Céline. The sun was shining, and fun and laughter were bubbling up inside her. She was about to suggest a lively game of blind-man's buff, when Victoire came out of the kitchen door. She had her apron full of peas she was going to shell, and she carried a small tin bucket in which to drop them. She sat down on a little three-legged stool near the door and placed the bucket on the ground beside her.

Céline whispered to Thérèse, "Let us go over and talk to her about Léon. Then she will forget all about the peas. And just watch the fun!"

Thérèse was quite willing, so the two ran over to Victoire.

"Would you like us to help you, Victoire?" Céline asked sweetly.

"I wouldn't trust my good peas to a mischief-maker like you", answered Victoire.

Thérèse dropped down at her feet on the grass. But Céline danced a little jig around the stool. When she stopped for breath, she said, "And how is Léon, Victoire?"

"Poor lad, he is worried", sighed Victoire.

"Why?" asked Thérèse.

"It is because of his father", explained Victoire. "Léon's father says we cannot be married because I have no dowry. Most women have at least a small dowry—a little money with which to start their marriage. But I have none."

"Oh, that is too bad!" exclaimed Thérèse.

"His father is an old bear", Victoire complained. "But my Léon is quite different. He still wants to marry me," she added proudly, "even though I have nothing but the clothes on my back."

Céline began dancing another jig around the stool. She stopped behind Victoire and exclaimed, "Why, here's a four-leaf clover! I'll pick it for you, Victoire, and it will bring you and Léon good luck!"

Victoire was leaning toward Thérèse and saying, "That old bear thinks about nothing but money. But Léon says we shall not mind him. Just as soon as Léon has saved enough, we are to be married and make our own home."

"Oh, Victoire, what shall we ever do when you leave?" asked Thérèse. "It will be terrible without you."

"Oh, it's a long way off yet", answered Victoire as she reached down for the little tin bucket. But the bucket was gone.

"Now where *is* that bucket?" demanded Victoire. "Everything I put down in this garden disappears." And with that she jumped up to look around.

There was a great clatter. For with her she took both pail and stool. They were tied to her back by her apron strings. Already Céline was halfway across the garden, running toward the old oak tree.

Victoire snatched up a broom that stood by the door and was after her in a flash, waving the broom, and with the bucket and stool still clattering at her back.

"I'll fix you, you young mischief", she screamed at Céline, who had climbed on a limb of the oak tree, out of arm's reach. Victoire beat the broom against the lower branches, but she could not reach Céline.

"Why, Victoire," called Céline, "I only wanted to help you. You said you had nothing but the clothes on your back. So I only wanted to put something more on your back!"

Thérèse couldn't help giggling. Victoire did look very funny indeed, with a bucket and a stool hanging at her back. When Marie came out of the kitchen door, both Thérèse and Céline were doubled up with laughter.

"Thérèse, stop laughing at once", she said sharply.

"And you, Céline," Marie went on, "you naughty girl, come right down out of that tree and take those things off poor Victoire's back! And tell her that you are very sorry. At thirteen, you should have more sense. For this, you shall not go to your aunt's for supper tomorrow night. You will have to give up your turn to Léonie."

As Céline came slowly down the tree, Marie turned to Victoire. "My poor Victoire, I am so sorry", she said. "Never mind our young mischief. And I want you to ask Léon to stay for supper when he comes to see you tomorrow afternoon."

As Thérèse followed her sisters into the kitchen, she remembered how hurt she had been when the older girls at school laughed at her. She hurried back to Victoire and said, "I am so sorry. I did not mean to hurt you by laughing."

Victoire smiled broadly and gave Thérèse a quick hug.

Happy again, Thérèse scampered back to her sisters. She caught up with them in the sitting room, where Céline was looking at a new painting by Pauline.

Pauline had studied painting at school, and her father was very proud of her work. Many of her pictures hung in his room. Thérèse loved to sit at her side while she was painting and watch the skill with which she mixed the colors and made lovely pictures with her brush.

"If only I could learn to paint like Pauline!" she thought. "I *do* wish I could have some painting lessons."

Céline felt the same way. She was always trying to copy Pauline's pictures.

One evening when they were all at supper, her father turned to Céline with a smile. "I've planned to have you take painting lessons at the convent when the new term opens", he said.

Céline clapped her hands in delight.

Then Louis Martin looked at Thérèse. "And you, Little Queen, would you also like to take lessons?"

Before Thérèse could answer joyfully that she would, Marie said, "I think Thérèse is too young, Father, for those lessons. Besides, she hasn't the talent for painting that Céline has."

Thérèse opened her mouth to object. She knew that her father would give her anything she asked. She had only to speak, and the lessons would be hers. But suddenly a thought stopped her. If she tried very hard to be silent and say nothing, it would be a big sacrifice to offer to the Infant Jesus. So the small mouth closed again. It was awfully hard to keep it closed, but she did. And it was the biggest sacrifice she had yet made for him. She remembered that her mother had said she wanted *all* her girls to become saints. But it wasn't going to be easy, this being a saint. She wondered if she could ever become one.

Later that night, after she and Pauline had said the Rosary before our Lady's altar, Pauline put an arm about her. "I think you made a very great sacrifice at supper this evening", she said. "I was proud of you."

Thérèse was surprised and happy. She never dreamed that Pauline had noticed her struggle.

"If we could only have more time together," Pauline went on, "I would teach you to paint. But now that . . . ." She broke off suddenly, without finishing what she had started to say.

"Now that *what?*" asked Thérèse.

"Oh, nothing", answered her sister. "Or rather, it's a secret of mine. Someday I shall tell you."

As Thérèse fell asleep that night, she kept thinking about Pauline's secret. "I wonder what it can be?" she asked herself.

One night not many weeks later, when Céline and Thérèse were in bed, Pauline came in as usual to kiss them good-night.

"I have something to tell you both", she said, sitting down on the edge of Thérèse's bed. "Do you remember, Thérèse, that I told you I had a secret? Can you guess now what it is?"

Céline sat bolt upright in bed. "I can", she said. "You are going to be married, like Victoire!"

Pauline threw back her head and laughed.

"No", she said. "Or at least, not like Victoire."

"How then?" demanded Céline.

"Well, dear," answered Pauline, "you know that a nun is often called the bride of Christ."

"A *nun*?" they both cried at once.

"You both know our lovely convent of the Carmel here in Lisieux. Well, I will soon be a Carmelite nun inside those walls."

Thérèse did not know what came over her, but suddenly she buried her head on Pauline's shoulder and wept. She knew that the nuns of Carmel were very happy people. And, above all, she wanted Pauline to be happy. But how would she ever get along in life without her little mother? The Carmel behind the high hedge would take Pauline away from her completely.

As the summer days passed, Thérèse became more and more unhappy. She tried to talk it all over with the Infant Jesus. At first, he did not seem to listen. And then one day, when she was alone in the rose garden, she thought she heard him whisper, "You too must enter the Carmel."

She was so startled that she sat right down beside a big red rosebush and stayed there for a long time, thinking. For the next few days, the family noticed that she was very quiet.

At last she went to Pauline and said, "I too have decided to enter the Carmel."

"But Thérèse! This cannot be. You are only nine years old!"

"I know," answered Thérèse, "but I think the Infant Jesus wants me there. Please, Pauline dear, take me to see the reverend mother."

"But, dear, it won't do any good." Then, seeing the hurt look on her little sister's face, she added, "Well, I will take you to see her, for I would like you to meet her in any case."

When the reverend mother looked down into the earnest blue eyes and the young face framed in golden hair, she did not smile because one so young wanted to enter Carmel. There was something about this little girl—she did not know what it was.

"It may well be, my dear," she said to Thérèse, "that God has called you to us at this early age. But you know that the convent cannot allow one so young to enter. Go on with your prayers, asking God to guide you. When you are older, we shall talk again."

Thérèse went sadly away. How many years would she have to wait before they would let her enter Carmel? Just then, the years ahead of her looked endless.

At length, in October, came the day when Pauline

would leave for Carmel. Thérèse tried to keep back the tears, for everyone in the family was weeping—even her father. While they knew that they could visit her from time to time in the convent behind the high hedge, they also knew that she would never return home again. It was a sad day in the Martin house, and yet somehow they felt a certain happiness too. Thérèse looked down at her little beads of sacrifices. How small and worthless they now seemed! Pauline was making the great sacrifice.

Marie, Léonie, and Céline were proud of this sister who was so happily giving up all the pleasant things of the world. She was just twenty-one.

Aunt Céline, who led an active social life in Lisieux, had planned a busy winter for her pretty niece. But now she had to explain to her friends, "The Carmel has swallowed her up!"

Yet she too was proud of Pauline.

As soon as the last good-bye had been said, it seemed that her father and sisters went out of their way to please Thérèse. School had opened again, and her father was more cheerful than usual when he called for her and Céline. He kept them laughing at his stories all the way home. Victoire always had some hidden surprise for her in the kitchen, a special cake or some candy she had made just for her. They all seemed to know how much Thérèse missed her little mother, and they tried to make her happy. But Thérèse's smiles did not come as often these days.

Time at school dragged on endlessly. The teasing of the older girls seemed harder than ever to bear. While her marks were still high, she was having trouble with her arithmetic and spelling. If her little mother had been at home, she would have helped her. But Thérèse did not want to bother Marie and Léonie, both of whom had many extra duties now that Pauline was gone. Only in her free time in the garden, when she and Céline and Tom would romp and play, could she forget her sadness for a time.

Bad headaches began to bother her at the start of the new year. True to her promise to the Infant Jesus, she did not complain. But sometimes her head hurt so badly that she had to close her eyes over her books for a long time.

One evening just before Easter vacation, their father said to them, "I think it is time that we all had a holiday. Little Queen, how would you and Céline like to spend a week with your aunt and uncle?"

The two were delighted with the idea. But Thérèse asked, "Do you suppose that Aunt Céline would let us bring Tom?"

"Of course", said her father.

Then he turned to Marie and Léonie. "And you, my dears, what would you think of a little jaunt to Paris with your old father?"

"Paris! How wonderful!" they both cried at once.

Even Victoire was to have a holiday.

The day soon came when the family with their

bags and Tom piled into a carriage. The horses stopped first at the Guérin house, where Louis Martin left Céline and Thérèse with their aunt. She greeted them with open arms. Tom frisked about the Guérin girls, who were old friends of his, and enjoyed it when they petted him. Thérèse clung to her father for a long moment when he kissed her good-bye. Suddenly, she did not want him to go away.

"Don't be sad, Little Queen", he said, giving her an extra hug. "I will bring you something fine from Paris. And while I am there I will light a candle just for you at the Church of Our Lady of Victories."

Thérèse knew that Our Lady of Victories was a famous church in Paris, where through the years many prayers had been heard and many favors had been granted. Then they were all standing at the door, waving to the group in the carriage, as the horses started off for the railway station.

Their uncle, laughing and talking, took Céline and Thérèse by the hand and led them upstairs to the pretty bedroom they were to share. It opened right into the room of Jeanne and Marie. The four cousins were looking forward to some happy times together, and Aunt Céline had planned a party for them.

When they were at the table enjoying the good food fixed by Marcelline, Thérèse noticed that her uncle was staring at her. She loved this kind uncle, but it made her uneasy to see him watching her so closely. Had she done something to displease him? So after dinner, she said to him, "I hope you are not displeased with me, dear Uncle."

He put his arm about her and led her into his study. All the others had gone outside, for it was a warm day.

"Forgive me, Thérèse," he said, as he settled into his big chair, "if I have stared at you and made you feel uncomfortable. The truth is that you have grown so much like my dear sister, your mother, that I cannot keep from looking at you."

Thérèse blushed with pleasure. "Do I then look like my mother?" she asked.

"It is not so much that your face is like hers, but rather that your manner and your voice are like hers in every way. To see you at our table today carried me back many years. I loved your mother very dearly."

"Tell me about her when she was my age", begged Thérèse.

She dropped on a little stool at her uncle's feet and looked up at him. An hour slipped by as he talked of the old days in Alençon when Zélie Guérin was a little girl like Thérèse. He told her of their school and their play. He also mentioned later days, when her mother had become interested in making lace and had wanted to become a nun, like Pauline. But instead she had happily married Louis Martin. Thérèse could not help it, but soon she was weeping.

Memories of her babyhood in Alençon and of her mother's gentleness flooded her heart. Then suddenly, one of the awful headaches began. She thanked her uncle and went upstairs to wash away the tears. She would not tell anyone about her headaches.

But later that night, when everyone was in bed and the whole house was silent, Thérèse lay awake in the darkness, unable to sleep because of the pain in her head. Suddenly she felt so cold that she began to shiver.

"I will not call Céline", she said to herself. "I will just ask the Infant Jesus to make me feel better."

But instead of getting better, the pain became worse, and at last she was forced to call Céline. Her sister was out of bed in a flash and ran to call their aunt. All that night Thérèse tossed and moaned, while Aunt Céline sat at her bedside with cold water and towels, bathing her forehead. But in the morning, she was no better, and the doctor was called. She was very ill, and the doctor himself was puzzled. Day after day, all through the week, she lay there, too ill to know what was going on about her. Aunt Céline took care of her as if she had been her own child, but Thérèse grew no better. Everyone in the house was unhappy and worried. Everyone longed for Saturday to come, when Thérèse's father and the two older girls would return from Paris.

When Louis Martin walked into Thérèse's room,

he could not believe that the pale little girl in bed was his own Little Queen. Gently, he bent over her and kissed her. For a moment she knew him and smiled, but the next instant, she did not know him and began to cry.

Wrapped in blankets and in her father's arms, she was taken home in the carriage waiting outside. She was put in Marie's room, in Pauline's bed, so that her oldest sister could watch her through the night. At one end of the room stood Our Lady of the Smile, but Thérèse did not notice her. The awful headache stayed with her day after day, and she burned with fever. Dr. Notta came every day, but when the worried family gathered around him as he was leaving, he could only shake his head.

"It is a strange sickness", he said. "I am doing my best."

The days dragged on. Someone was always with her; if not her father, then Marie, Léonie, or Céline. Poor Victoire climbed the stairs from the kitchen three times a day with trays of good food. Thérèse only pushed them from her. Léonie took over the task of seeing that there was always fresh cold water beside Thérèse. She would slip her arm under her sister's head and hold the glass to her lips when she saw that Thérèse was burning with fever. News of Thérèse's sickness was sent to Pauline in the convent, and at once all the Carmelite nuns began praying for the sick child.

She grew no better. She did not know where she was, or who these strange people were who stayed near her. They frightened her. Where was her father? Where were her sisters? Why did they not come and take her away from this terrible place? Why did they not take her home?

Once, to Marie's joy, she seemed to grow better for a few hours, and she called Marie by name. She even turned her head toward our Lady and held out her arms as if she were begging for help. But within a short time she was tossing and moaning again.

Now she had become Joan of Arc, leading the armies of France to victory. Then the walls of the room seemed to be marching toward her. In a moment they would reach her bed and crush her. She cried out in fear and hid her face in her hands. Again, a nail in the wall began to grow and spread as she watched. Suddenly it took the shape of a horrible black hand. Its fingers were reaching out to clutch her. She shook with terror and hid her head under the covers.

One afternoon, her father returned from the Carmel where he had gone to beg for extra prayers. In his hurry to see if there had been any change, he ran up the stairs with his hat in his hand. As he came near the bed, Thérèse began to tremble. Then she noticed the hat he was holding. But now it wasn't a hat at all. It was a huge spider coming toward her. As the black, hairy legs reached out for her face, she gave a terrified scream and fell back on the pillows, unconscious—her body rigid and her face white.

Louis Martin fell on his knees at the foot of the bed and buried his face in his hands. Great sobs shook him. Now he knew that his little Thérèse was dying.

5

A LADY SMILES

ON THE TOPMOST floor of the house was a large room from whose windows could be seen many miles of the beautiful French countryside. When the Martins had moved to Lisieux, the girls had carefully furnished this room as a study for their father. They wanted it to take the place of his beloved Pavilion in Alençon. Here, away from the noises of the house, he could read and rest and be alone with his thoughts.

Louis Martin sat there now, with his head in his hands. Thérèse was dying.

Well, if that was God's will, he would accept it. His mind went back over the years to all those he had loved and who had been taken from him. In the early days of his marriage, there had been the four little children whose death had caused him and his wife so much sadness. Then there had been his beloved Zélie herself. He had thought that his five daughters would be spared to him. But Pauline had entered the convent. And now his dearest, the baby of the family, at the age of ten was to be taken from him. He had written to Paris to ask for special prayers at the Church of Our Lady of Victories, but it seemed that they were not to be answered.

"Dear God," he prayed, "give me the grace to accept your will, whatever it may be."

But his heart was breaking.

Downstairs in the sickroom, Thérèse had opened her eyes. Marie, standing there full of worry, bathed her face gently in cold water. Thérèse drew back from her, not knowing who she was. Presently, the doctor came and sat at her bed for a time. When he arose to go, he called Marie into the hall.

"She is worse today", he said. "I fear . . . ." He did not finish, but Marie understood. Her heart stood still.

"Shall I call Father?" she asked.

"No", replied the doctor. "I do not think it will happen today. Better to let him rest while he can."

Léonie came softly into the sickroom, so Marie went down to the door with the doctor. After he had gone, she slipped out into the garden for a moment. It was a warm day in May, and she felt as though she were going to faint. The fresh air would help. She was standing right under the window of the sickroom when she heard Thérèse call to her.

"Marie, Marie!" came the suffering little voice through the open window.

In a flash, Marie was running up the stairs. "Here I am, dear", she said as she dashed to the bedside.

But Thérèse did not know her. She looked fearfully at her and kept on calling "Marie!" She appeared to be in great pain.

With tears running down her face, Marie dropped to her knees before the altar of Our Lady of the Smile. Céline had slipped into the room, and she and Léonie knelt down beside Marie. Aloud they prayed with all their hearts that our Lady would ask her Son to let Thérèse stay with them.

Thérèse weakly turned her head on the pillow and saw them there. A flash of memory returned. She knew all at once that they were her sisters, and that they were praying for her. Lying there in great suffering, she raised her eyes to the statue, and she too begged our Lady for help.

Then strangely, as Thérèse prayed, the statue disappeared. A wonderfully beautiful Lady had taken its place. And the Lady was smiling down at her with a smile whose sweetness Thérèse was to remember all the days of her life. The Lady held out her arms. And as she did so, suddenly all the pain went away. It was as though a hand had lifted away a great load that had been resting on the sick child's forehead. Thérèse was cured.

In the happy days that followed, someone about the house was always singing. Marie hummed as she went about her tasks. Léonie and Céline sang together. And Louis Martin poured out his fine voice in the old French songs he loved. Even Victoire, as she worked in the kitchen, sang love songs over her pots and pans.

"Thinking of Léon?" Céline would ask, sticking her head in the door. Victoire would just flick a dish towel at her and go right on singing.

Thérèse was cured. The soft summer breeze blew through the open windows and fluttered the pretty curtains. Out in the garden, bright flowers were bowing and smiling to one another. Thérèse still lay upstairs in her bed, gathering strength after the long illness. But her mind was clear again, and all the pain had gone away. Dr. Notta was delighted, but he could not explain the cure. For now Thérèse knew everyone who came into the room, and she was so happy to see them.

Victoire said, "At last she is eating my good food again. *That* will make her well!"

Even Tom seemed a different dog. For weeks he had lain sadly at the sickroom door, all the fun gone out of him. Now he was allowed to come in and frisk about Thérèse's bed and to lick her hand. She was very glad to see him.

Once when she and Marie were alone, Marie said to her, "Dear, I should not ask, and you need not tell me if you do not wish. But what *did* happen, that afternoon when the rest of us were praying at our Lady's altar?"

Thérèse was silent, but a look of great happiness came over her face.

"I *know* something happened," Marie went on, "because from where I knelt, I could see you plainly. For such a long time, my poor dear, your eyes had been dull. They saw nothing. But just at the moment when I glanced at you, suddenly you lifted yourself on the pillow. Your eyes opened wide, and life came back to them. Such a look of happiness I shall never forget. It was as if the sun were playing over your face. You were gazing at the statue, as though something wonderful were happening there. But I could see nothing unusual."

Thérèse lay silent for a long moment. Then she said simply, "Our Lady of the Smile came to life and smiled on me. Oh, she was so beautiful, Marie! And then, all at once, the pain stopped, and I knew that I was cured."

Now within a short time, Thérèse was out in the garden again and even skipping rope, with Tom frisking about and barking at her flying heels. The roses were very beautiful this year, and she kept our Lady's altar glowing with them. But every time she bent to cut one, she could not help whispering to it, "I hope this does not hurt you very much."

For the altar of the Infant Jesus, she had planted a special bed of lilies of the valley. She thought that he would like them best because they were tiny little flowers for a tiny little Infant.

Marie Guérin, who had missed her cousin at school during the long weeks, now came every day to play with her. Louis Martin was often in the garden with them, seated with a book in his hands. But his eyes were on Thérèse more often than they were on his book. He was watching to see the color come back into her cheeks. Although he had said nothing about it, he planned to take her on a little trip when she was strong enough to travel.

One morning at breakfast about a week later, he said to his daughters, "Well, young ladies, pack your bags today, for tomorrow we are going on a trip."

Cries of excitement and delight went up. "Where, Father?" the girls chorused.

"To Alençon", he replied. "We shall have a little holiday there among our old friends."

Céline jumped up and did a little dance around the table. Thérèse clapped her hands. Marie laughed delightedly.

"But where are we to stay? Our Pavilion is not big enough to hold all of us!" Léonie exclaimed.

"Of course not", her father answered. "The Pavilion, as you know by now, is for gentlemen only. So Tom and I shall put up there."

"Oh, goody!" cried Thérèse. "We are taking Tom!"

"Indeed we are", replied her father. "You don't think I could manage four girls by myself, do you?"

"But where are we to stay?" asked his two older daughters.

"You two have been invited to stay with your mother's old friend, Madame Tifenne. Céline and Thérèse will stay with another old friend, Mademoiselle Romet."

"Oh, what fun!" they all cried at once. For they well remembered these two family friends who had loved their mother. Both had lovely homes in Alençon.

"They have been writing me for some time," their father went on, "asking us to visit them. And I thought now would be a good time."

The house was in a flutter all day long, as the girls prepared for their trip. Victoire went about grumbling, as she washed the pretty summer dresses and ironed them, complaining that there was not enough time to do her work properly.

"Don't grumble, dear Victoire", said Céline. "Just think, you are to have a holiday too, and you can see your Léon every day. Maybe you'll be married by the time we return!"

"It is true that I shall be able to see more of Léon", agreed Victoire. "But as for marriage, that old bear, his father, would not allow it now. And poor Léon has not yet saved enough."

"If you will light a candle at our Lady's altar," said Thérèse, "and pray every day, I know she will find a way for you and Léon to be married."

That night, just before she went up to bed, Thérèse went over to her father's chair and whispered in his ear, "While we are in Alençon, Father dear, shall we be able to make a little visit to our mother's grave?"

"Of course", answered her father, putting his arm about her. "That is part of our plan."

Next morning at an early hour, the family drove off to the railway station, waving good-bye to Victoire, who stood flapping her apron at them. When they arrived in Alençon some hours later, they took a carriage that first dropped Marie and Léonie at Madame Tifenne's home. Then it took Céline and Thérèse to Mademoiselle Romet's. Finally it stopped at the Pavilion to leave Louis Martin and Tom.

Then began a most exciting two weeks. The plump Madame Tifenne was a kindly, rich widow. She had told all her friends that Marie and Léonie would be with her for a time. Since Marie was now twenty-three and Léonie twenty, they were invited with Madame Tifenne to a number of parties and dances. Their father, who was invited also, was proud of his two tall and lovely daughters.

Mademoiselle Romet, who had Céline and Thérèse under her roof, was a jolly lady from a fine old family. She had planned happy times for the younger girls. There were picnics and parties and drives around the lovely countryside. Some of her relatives had beautiful homes near Alençon, and she was asked to bring her young guests to parties at these homes.

After lunch, the boys and girls in these households would take Céline and Thérèse out to the tennis courts or to the stables for rides on their ponies. Thérèse loved the ponies, and Céline, who was now thirteen, wanted to learn to play tennis.

At one beautiful old home, with lovely gardens stretching all about it, there were two young people. Margot was ten, like Thérèse, and she enjoyed taking her new friend through the gardens and down to the river, where there was a little boat house. They went rowing near the shore and picked the flowers that grew there.

Charles, Margot's brother, was a tall boy of fifteen with big black eyes. He was just two years older than Céline. He was very polite and offered to teach Céline to play tennis. They were invited often to this home, and Mademoiselle Romet noticed that Charles was very attentive to Céline.

"Your sister has an admirer", she whispered to Thérèse, with a twinkle in her eye.

After that, Thérèse wanted to laugh every time she saw Charles looking at Céline. His big eyes reminded her of Tom's when he was begging for a bone. But Céline did not seem to notice this, and she was always making them laugh with her pranks. As the sun was setting after a happy day, the Martin girls would drive home with Mademoiselle Romet.

Every morning, Louis Martin would call for Céline and Thérèse. They would go for a walk along the old streets the girls had known as little children. Sometimes they spent the morning in the garden of their beloved Pavilion. Often they went to visit their mother's grave and to lay flowers upon it.

Kneeling there, Thérèse prayed with all her heart to her mother, asking her help in making more sacrifices for the Infant Jesus. She fingered the beads in her pocket and whispered, "There are only two, so far today. You know I must do better than that!"

On Sunday, they went to the Church of Notre Dame, which Thérèse had so greatly loved when she was a tiny girl. In the late afternoon they returned for Vespers. Thérèse felt exactly as she had when she was very small. The beautiful colors of the old windows, the music, and the candles filled her with happiness and peace. On their way back, Louis Martin told them, as he had so often told them before, of the time Thérèse had run away in the storm and tried to find her way to this church.

During their visit in Alençon, they walked past their old house, so full of memories, happy and sad. But they did not go in, as another family was living there now.

When they returned to Lisieux, they all felt better for their holiday. And Louis Martin, seeing that Thérèse's cheeks were rosy again, was well pleased.

Victoire was in the kitchen fixing supper when they came home, and Céline and Thérèse ran out to greet her there. She hugged them both and then stood with her hands on her hips, admiring them.

"Why, you look almost like grown-up young ladies!" she exclaimed. "You must tell me all that you did in Alençon."

"And what about you?" asked Céline. "You didn't marry Léon while we were gone?"

"Of course not", said Victoire crossly. "Do you think that such things are done so quickly?"

"Well," said Céline teasingly, "we would have taken you with us to Alençon, but we *knew* that you would never leave your Léon."

"Don't mind her, Victoire", said Thérèse. "She can't tease you any more about Léon. You just ask her about *her* new admirer!"

"Ho, ho", said Victoire, laughing. "So that's it!"

"His name is Charles, and he lives in a big house

near the river", went on Thérèse, as Céline grew more and more uncomfortable. "And this is how he looks at Céline."

Then she stood very straight on tiptoe, made a solemn face, and opened her eyes very wide as she gazed at her sister. She managed to look so much like Charles that even Céline had to laugh.

When school opened in the fall, Thérèse was told that she would be allowed to make her First Holy Communion in May. In the following weeks, Thérèse would bring her catechism to Marie every evening after supper. Together they would go up to her father's study on the top floor where all was quiet. There Marie taught her carefully and prepared her to receive our Lord.

Then one day she was told that she would spend the last week before her First Communion at the convent. She and the other girls who would receive Communion with her were to stay there in retreat. She was to sleep there, and she would not see her family again for seven long days and nights. Thérèse was frightened. Never before had she slept away from some member of her family. What would the convent be like at night? Would the older girls tease her? What would Francine do to her? But still, when the day came, she went with courage, for she knew that at the end of the week she would receive the Infant Jesus. And for that, she was ready to go through anything.

When she reached the convent with her little bag, she found it was quite different from what she had feared. This convent was a huge place, and now she was led to a part of it she had never seen before. It lay far away from the school. No one was there except the nuns and the other girls who were going into retreat. A kind priest named Father Domin came every day to speak with them. They spent much time in the chapel, praying or listening to special talks. They walked in the grounds while the other children were in school. And most of the time they kept silence. Although she knew that Céline and Marie Guérin were there in class every day, Thérèse never saw them.

More and more of her thoughts went up to God. But sometimes she could not help but think also of what happy times awaited her at home. Victoire had told her that Marie had planned a family party for her at which she would be given presents. And although she was not supposed to do so, Victoire had not been able to resist whispering also that her father had bought Thérèse a beautiful little gold watch, all for her own, as his special present to her. Best of all, he himself had promised her that in the afternoon they would visit Pauline in the Carmelite Convent, so that Pauline could see Thérèse in her new white dress and her First Communion veil. Thérèse thought what a wonderful family God had given to her, and she thanked him.

At night she slept in a little bed behind drawn curtains. She never felt homesick, for every night the reverend mother came with a flickering candle in her hand to kiss her good-night. Every day she grew happier as she felt the Infant Jesus drawing closer and closer.

It seemed that, gently as a dove, a new light had come to rest upon her thoughts. No longer did she picture herself becoming another Joan of Arc, leader of France. She saw that she was meant to be little Thérèse of Lisieux—Thérèse of no great courage, of no great gift, of no great strength. For all her deep love, she knew now that she could never become a great warrior for God and for France. She would not do well on the battlefield. God had not made her for that. She was meant to serve him in another way.

Joan of Arc had been the lily of France that had stood, beautiful and tall and strong, upon a strong stem. But Thérèse was rather like one of the small wildflowers she had so often come upon when she and her father and Tom had walked through the fields. How often she had stopped to gather them! They grew small and weak, hidden by the tall grasses around them. They weren't strong at all, for when you picked them they soon died in your hands. Yet, lovely in color and form, they grew only to praise God who had made them. She was far more like these than she was like the strong, beautiful lily of France. So at her First Holy Communion, she would ask God not for the greatness of the lily but only for the hidden simple place of a little flower of the field. She would ask to live and to grow only by grace of his love.

At last the great day dawned. Marie herself came to the convent to dress her. She placed a crown of small white roses upon her little sister's head. As Thérèse walked into the chapel with the other girls, she knew that her father and all the family, even Victoire—all except Pauline—were there for the Mass. As the time for Communion drew near, her knees began to tremble. Would they carry her as far as the altar rail? All at once she found herself kneeling there.

Then as she walked away with folded hands and bent head, suddenly the trembling stopped, and she felt a great peace. Angels' wings fluttered above and about her. Something within her was singing with a strange, sweet music she had never heard before.

6

SEASHORE AND SACRIFICE

ON AN AUGUST morning of the year 1886, Thérèse and her cousin Marie were perched upon a big rock high above the beach of Trouville. Below them, the blue sea with the sunlight dancing upon it rolled endlessly and flowed in upon the white sands. As far as they could look, there was nothing but sun and sea and sky.

Marcelline, the Guérin's maid, sat on a rock some yards away, knitting busily. Every once in a while she would raise her eyes toward her charges, the two cousins. For although Thérèse was now thirteen and Marie all of sixteen, young girls of France never went anywhere unless an older person was with them.

How pretty the two looked in their bright summer dresses with the breeze playing through their curls, thought Marcelline—Thérèse, with the golden hair and big blue eyes, and Marie, with her dark curls and large black eyes.

They were laughing at Tom, who was frisking about and racing after the red ball they were throwing to him. Just then, Marie threw the ball a little too far, and it rolled to the edge of the rock and over it and down upon the beach below. The two girls leaned over the rock to watch Tom scramble down onto the white sand. Tom searched wildly among the bathers for his ball.

"Oh, look", cried Thérèse. "Tom has found Céline and Jeanne!"

She pointed to the brightly colored umbrella about which Tom was now frisking. Aunt Céline was there with a group of young people, among whom were Céline and Jeanne. Céline was now rolling Tom over in the sand.

"Look at the young man sitting next to Jeanne", said Marie. "That's the one."

"Oh, Marie, do you really think that Jeanne is

going to marry him?" asked Thérèse, as she looked at him curiously.

"Well, his parents have called upon our parents, and he has already asked her to marry him. And Jeanne is now eighteen, you know."

"It must be very hard to be eighteen", said Thérèse. "Everyone expects you to get married."

"I heard Mother and Father tell Jeanne that it would be a good match. He's a young doctor. His name is André—Dr. André La Néele."

Thérèse and Céline had arrived only last evening for a visit with the Guérins. Thérèse had not been well this summer, and Aunt Céline thought the sea air would do her good. This morning, high upon the sunny rock, Marie had been giving her cousin all the latest family news. The Guérins had come to Trouville for the season. Thérèse's two older sisters, Marie and Léonie, had stayed at home with their father. But Louis Martin was joining Thérèse and Céline for the weekend. He would arrive with Monsieur Guérin, who had been in Lisieux on business. Aunt Céline had planned a happy weekend for all of them at the Guérin's house.

"I'm so happy that your father is coming!" exclaimed Marie. "I do love him. He is my favorite uncle."

"And your father is mine!" exclaimed Thérèse.

Then they both laughed, as they realized that each of them had but one uncle apiece.

"I mean," said Marie, "that if I did have any *other* uncles, Uncle Louis would still be my favorite."

"He loves to have you play for him on the piano", said Thérèse. "And he loves to hear you sing. He thinks you have a beautiful voice."

"Well, so has he", said Marie. "But I wonder why he always calls me his little Greek girl."

"Because of your big black eyes", explained Thérèse.

"I think that I love him most because he is so good", said Marie. "I don't believe I ever knew anyone as good as Uncle Louis. And then besides, he is so handsome with his white hair."

Thérèse agreed happily. And then she said, "I love your father, too. Since we were little, he has always given us the loveliest presents. But I think I love him most because he is my mother's brother. He loved her so much and has told me so much about her."

"He says that you are very like her", remarked Marie.

"But, oh, Marie, whatever would we Martin girls have done without your mother!" exclaimed Thérèse. "Aunt Céline has been a true mother to us since we lost our own."

"Then that makes us true sisters", said Marie, smiling. "I've felt that way ever since you started school at the convent."

"And I have too, from that moment when you

first defended me against Francine and the older girls!" exclaimed Thérèse.

"It shall be that way all through our lives", said Marie. "I want you to share everything I have. And do you know, Thérèse, that one day we shall be very rich, you and I?"

"Why, no", answered Thérèse, opening her eyes wide.

"Marcelline was telling me the other day," went on Marie, "something she probably should not have been telling me. But it was that a great deal of money and a large home with beautiful gardens will belong to my father when his older cousin dies. The money doesn't matter, but the home is so beautiful, Thérèse! I've been there on visits. It's circled by a lovely park, and *you* will lose your mind over the gardens!"

"How wonderful that will be for you and Jeanne!" exclaimed Thérèse.

"For you and me, is what I was thinking", said Marie. "For Jeanne will soon be married. Then you Martins will all come to live with us there, and you and I shall share everything like the true sisters we are. We shall be great ladies, and we shall have horses and dogs and everything we want."

Thérèse was gazing dreamily far out over the sea stretching beneath them. For a moment she was silent, and then she said, pressing her cousin's hand, "I love you for having such thoughts. But, dear

Marie, forgive me—there is something I want far more than riches and a beautiful home."

Marie turned her head and looked at her. "I think", she said softly, "I can guess what *that* is."

"Yes, I'm sure that you have guessed it", answered Thérèse. "It's the Carmel, of course."

"Because Pauline is there?" asked Marie.

"Oh no", answered Thérèse. "Not because of Pauline. When I enter, I shall see very little of her. You know how it is in the Carmel. One is not allowed to have any special friend among the other nuns. In fact, I think that Pauline and I will see no more of each other there than we do now."

"Then why?" pressed Marie.

"Because ever since I was nine, I have known that the Infant Jesus wants me there", explained Thérèse simply. "And ever since my First Communion, I have known it constantly. Marie, I want to go there at once!"

"But dear, at *thirteen*? It is much too young to be accepted as a nun!" said Marie.

"I suppose so", said Thérèse unhappily. "But I've been waiting for such a long time."

"Did you never want to do anything else?" her cousin asked.

"Oh yes! When I was small I dreamed of doing great deeds for God and France. You will laugh, Marie, but I wanted to be a great leader like Joan of Arc."

"That is not so strange", said her cousin.

"And then later, how much I longed to travel all over the world for God as a missionary! I wanted to win many souls for him. I wanted to die for him as a martyr. I wanted to show my love for him by giving up everything for him."

"Well, isn't that the way?" asked Marie.

"Yes", answered Thérèse. "But our Lady, who came to smile on me when I was ill, taught me many new things. She taught me first that I am not strong enough to be a Joan of Arc, not even strong enough to be a missionary. After that illness, Marie, I have known that I would never be really strong again. I will be ill much of the time. And I will not live long."

"Hush, Thérèse!" exclaimed Marie. "How can you say such things? It is all in God's hands."

"But this, I think, God wanted me to know," said Thérèse, "so that I could use the few years that are left in the way that would please him most—in sacrifice."

"The Carmel is sacrifice", agreed Marie.

"That is why I want to enter it more than any other convent. There the nuns live and die, unknown to the world. When I received my First Communion, the Infant Jesus showed me how all God's children are really his flowers. The world is like a great garden, full of all sorts of flowers. Some, like Joan of Arc, are like beautiful lilies, for whom

God has some special, great purpose. Others, like myself, are like the tiny, unseen field flowers. I am only a *little* flower. Others, like you, to whom God has given a special beauty, are like roses. I think he must love the roses best of all, for he has made them the most beautiful. You are like a rose, with your strength and beauty and your music. You are a rose in God's garden!"

"I would say a dandelion," laughed Marie, "if not something less!"

"So now you see, dear Marie, why I am in such a hurry to enter the Carmel. I cannot wait longer. And just as soon as Father gets here, I am going to ask him to let me enter right away."

"He will say that you are too young", insisted Marie. "And after having given Pauline to the Carmel, he will not want to part with you."

"I know", said Thérèse sadly. "But he will come to see it my way. And when I become a Carmelite nun, Marie, this little flower will pray for you in your great home where you will be as graceful and as beautiful as a rose."

"How proud I shall be, to have *two* cousins who are Carmelites!" exclaimed Marie. "Have you thought yet about the name you will choose as a nun?"

"Oh yes", replied Thérèse. "I've thought a lot about it. I like my own name of Thérèse because it's the name of a very great saint whom I love, Teresa of Avila. She was so strong! She was one of the lilies, like Joan of Arc, born to do great things. I would like to keep her name, and add something to it. I should like to be called Sister Thérèse of the Child Jesus."

"A beautiful name!" cried Marie.

"But please never tell anyone," begged Thérèse, "that is, not until I have really won it. The Carmelites would think it very forward of me to choose a name even before I have been admitted!"

"I shall not tell", promised Marie.

Just then they heard Marcelline calling. She had risen from the rock where she had been sitting and was waving her knitting at them.

"Time to return for lunch", she cried. "And we must hurry, for that girl I left in the kitchen won't have any idea what to do unless I'm there to show her!"

On the walk back, Thérèse and Marcelline talked gaily, but Marie was very quiet. Just as they entered the garden, Marie pressed Thérèse's arm and whispered, "I envy you."

When Friday evening came and the two fathers were expected, each girl put on her prettiest dress. Thérèse tried to hide an excitement that made her heart beat very fast. At last, the time had come for which she had waited so long. Tonight, after dinner, she would beg her father to let her enter the convent behind the high hedge. She must find a quiet spot where they could talk. And she prayed very hard to the Infant Jesus, asking him to make the way smooth.

Aunt Céline had planned a special dinner and had invited Jeanne's admirer, the young doctor.

The two fathers came at about six o'clock, and the four girls rushed down the stairs to greet them. Louis Martin hugged Thérèse and then held her out at arm's length, looking her up and down.

"The sea air has brought the roses back to your cheeks, Little Queen", he said.

Her uncle caught her up in his arms. "Why, this young lady could never have been sick", he cried. "She looks as fresh as a daisy."

But somehow her father did not seem quite himself. He was more quiet than usual. Was he merely tired? Or had something gone wrong at home? Thérèse was troubled.

At the table there was much laughter, and after dinner Marie Guérin sat down at the piano. She played the music her uncle loved, and Thérèse noticed that under its spell her father brightened. Soon he and Marie were singing a song together. When the music was over, everyone clapped.

A little later, Thérèse slipped over to her father and whispered, "Will you go for a walk with me in the garden?"

The two stepped out into the warm night. They found themselves looking up at a sky full of stars. It was a beautiful summer evening, and father and daughter paused to breathe in the perfume of the flowers. They could hear the soft swish of the sea, as the waves rolled in upon the beach far below them.

"This is the moment," thought Thérèse, "for God is very close to us now."

But as they started to stroll down a garden path, before she could speak, her father had taken her arm and was saying, "I'm glad you suggested this. There is something important that I wanted to tell you."

"Oh, nothing unhappy, Father?" Thérèse quickly asked.

"Well, in a way it is", he answered. "It's about your big sister, Marie."

"Oh, she's not ill?" cried Thérèse.

"No, I left her quite well, keeping an eye on the house, as usual. She and Léonie are both quite well and sent you and Céline a great deal of love."

"What, then?" asked Thérèse, puzzled.

"She will enter the Carmel in October", said Louis Martin.

Thérèse clutched her father's arm and then sat down suddenly on a garden bench. "Marie—Carmel!" were the only words she could say. The very ground seemed to shake beneath her. Why this—this would change everything. She, Thérèse, was the one who should be entering the Carmel! Not Marie! She had thought of it first. She was sure she had.

"Why, dear, what's the matter?" asked her father, sitting down beside her and taking her hand. "You should not feel so sad, although I must admit, it has been a terrible blow to me."

"But Marie—she *can't*! Are you *sure*, Father? Is Marie sure?" asked Thérèse.

"Quite sure, my dear", he replied. "She told me that she has been wanting to take this step for a very long time, for many years, in fact."

"But she never told us", said Thérèse, trying to hold back the tears.

"No. She has been very brave", said Louis Martin.

"But why . . . ?"

"She wanted to fulfill the task that fell to her upon your mother's death", he answered. "She was the oldest child. She had to bring up her younger sisters and keep house for me and look after me. And she has done her task nobly", said Louis Martin.

"Indeed she has", agreed Thérèse, faintly.

"She was only seventeen when your mother died", her father went on. "She was only a young girl. And suddenly she had to become a woman overnight, a woman whose task it was to bring up four little sisters and to take care of a big household."

"She has been so good, Father, the best big sister who ever lived! Only . . . ." Thérèse's voice trailed off.

"I know", sighed Louis Martin. "We shall miss her terribly. But we cannot stand in her way. All this time, she has sacrificed herself for her family. But this thing she has wanted to do for a long time. She waited for you, the youngest, to grow up. When you reached the age of thirteen, she knew that you would no longer need her as you did when you were a child."

"Dear Marie!" cried Thérèse from a full heart.

"It is time that she should do what she wants. She will soon be twenty-seven years old. She has sacrificed many years for us." He sighed and put a hand over his eyes.

All at once Thérèse knew that her father was suffering deeply. How could she sit there, thinking of her own sadness, when her father was so unhappy? She had known that she would have to make a great sacrifice for the Infant Jesus as proof of her love. But she had never dreamed that it would be this!

She put her arms about her father.

"Do not feel so sad, Father dear", she begged him. "I will try to take Marie's place."

He patted her arm gratefully. But again he sighed. "The Carmel took our Pauline", he reminded her. "And now it is taking Marie. It is hard to give up two of my daughters—the two oldest. But since God has asked this sacrifice of me, I wish to make it gladly. Now, there will be only three of you left at home. Only Léonie, Céline, and my Little Queen. I pray that God will spare you all to me for a long time!"

Thérèse felt her heart breaking within her. She would not, she could not, leave her father now. Her secret must still remain untold.

As they arose to go indoors, they met Jeanne and her young man coming into the garden. The light from the lamps within fell full upon the faces of father and daughter.

"Why, Uncle Louis," exclaimed Jeanne, "you look tired! And you too, Thérèse dear! You must get some rest while you are with us. We want you to be feeling well and happy for our wedding." She turned happily toward her fiancé. "Don't we, André dear?" she asked.

7

THE CLOSED DOOR

CÉLINE and Thérèse returned from the seashore
in early September. Since then, Thérèse had
been more thoughtful of her father than ever. She
was with him on all his daily walks and on all his
fishing trips.

She was at home more these days than she had
been since she was a little girl. For in spite of the

good sea air of Trouville, her health was still poor. When school had opened, her father had decided not to let her return. It was too long a trip back and forth every day. Instead, she was to learn her lessons from a private teacher.

Céline, who had finished school, was now seventeen and quite a young lady. Louis Martin was happy with four of his daughters about him—Marie, Léonie, Céline, and Thérèse. He tried to forget that within a few weeks he would give up one of them to the convent behind the high hedge.

On an afternoon in late September, when the family was having tea, they heard the bell sound at the front door. Presently Victoire appeared in her white apron, looking wide-eyed and excited. She told the family, "It is a young gentleman who is calling on Céline. He says he is from Alençon and asks if she will remember Charles who played tennis with her there."

The whole family was surprised. It had been three years since Céline and Thérèse had visited Alençon and had been taken to Charles' home, where he had taught Céline to play tennis.

Louis Martin went out to greet the young man and to bring him in to the family circle. The tall Charles with the big black eyes was handsomer than ever. He was now eighteen.

He bowed to each of the girls, and then he said to Céline, "I was afraid you had forgotten me. Being on a visit to Lisieux, I hoped you would not mind if I called."

They at once made the young man feel at home, and Victoire brought in a fresh cup of tea. Thérèse smiled when she noticed that Charles was looking at Céline just as he had looked at her during that summer three years before.

When he got up to leave, he said to her father, "I shall be in Lisieux with friends for a few weeks. I hope I may call again."

"Of course," answered Louis Martin. "We shall be glad to see you."

Now it was Victoire's chance to tease Céline, who was always teasing *her* about her Léon. Charles called often and sometimes arrived when the family was out. At such times he would leave with Victoire a bunch of flowers or a box of candy for Céline. These gifts Victoire hid away in the kitchen until just the right moment, when all the family was together. Then she would enter with Charles' gift and take it over to Céline, saying in a loud voice, "Your admirer left this for you."

Then Marie and Léonie and Thérèse would tease Céline until she was very uncomfortable.

"Whatever makes him do this?" she would ask. "I wish he would go back to Alençon."

A few days before Marie was to leave for the convent, she said to her father, "Now soon, Father dear, when I go, my duties here must fall to one of the others. I have tried to teach each one how to keep house. Which one will you choose for your housekeeper? Léonie, Céline, or Thérèse?"

"Why, my good Léonie, of course," answered her father. "She will be the oldest one left at home."

Léonie looked startled. "Oh, Father," she said, "I should be glad, but you know that I would not be as good at it as the others. I seem to forget things so easily. Don't you remember the time when I had to get supper and boiled the dishcloth right in with the soup?"

Then they all laughed as they recalled that evening. Louis Martin had sat at the head of the table, dipping out the onion soup and praising Léonie for her cooking. All at once he dipped out a dishcloth with the soup. Léonie had blushed to the roots of her hair.

"That was long ago," said her father, "and since then you have become a very wise young lady. But to tell you the truth, I would rather have you go ahead with your good work for the poor of Lisieux than keep house for me."

For some months, Léonie had been visiting certain old ladies in the city who were poor and ill. She brought them food every day and spent long hours taking care of them. She seemed to be happiest when she was helping those who were suffering.

Just then, as Victoire entered with a platter of chicken, Louis Martin turned to Céline and said,

"When Marie leaves us, you, Céline, shall manage the house."

Victoire almost dropped the platter. "You mean," she gasped, "that I shall have to take orders from *that* harum-scarum?"

Everyone laughed but Victoire.

Then Céline said, "Don't worry, Victoire. I'll promise not to tease you, and I shall ask your advice about everything. You are much wiser than I. And just think how much you can teach me!"

Now Victoire was smiling again.

On the day Marie left for the convent, the whole family went with her in the carriage. As they kissed her tearfully at the gate, she said, "You are not to weep, for I am entering into great happiness. How much I shall be praying for all of you behind these walls!"

Then she turned to Céline. "Now don't forget to see that Father has some good apple jelly this winter, and in the spring, plenty of vegetables.'"

Her father could not help but think how much the Carmel would gain in this fine, practical daughter of his. Wherever she was, she would always be very helpful.

"Father dear," she was saying, "if they don't take good care of you, just send them around to see me!"

Then she was off up the path, and the door had closed upon her.

As they drove home, each trying to cheer the

other, Louis Martin thought sadly, "Now those walls have swallowed two of my daughters. It is hard. Yet I am proud that they are giving their lives to God."

That night, Thérèse prayed for a long time. "O Little Jesus, will my turn never come?" she asked. "I have been waiting for almost five years."

Tomorrow, she would talk it all over again with Céline. For she had told Céline, as well as her cousin Marie Guérin, about her wish to enter the Carmel. Every evening, the two sisters went up to the big room on the top floor to watch the sunset together. There Thérèse poured out all her thoughts to Céline. They would stand at the window looking out over the peaceful fields and hills, spread out like a great map below them. Somehow the sunsets seemed to bring them closer to God.

As they stood there the next evening, Céline said to Thérèse, "You have been brave, not to tell Father of your longing to enter Carmel. It is better to wait. All day there have been tears in his eyes over Marie."

"I know, I know", murmured Thérèse unhappily. "I would not cause him any more pain."

"And besides," Céline went on, "the Carmel would never admit you now. They would say that you are still a child. You won't be fourteen until January."

"Sometimes they admit girls at fifteen", said Thérèse hopefully.

"Not often", Céline reminded her. "And besides, it will be more than a year before you are fifteen."

During the summer that followed, Louis Martin often sat under the trees in his garden, thinking about his five daughters. The two oldest were now in Carmel. They were very religious, all his daughters. Their mother had trained them to be so. She had wanted all of them to become saints. He did, too. But could not one become a saint and yet remain in the world? His Zélie had remained in the world, had married, and had her children. She had been as nearly a saint as anyone he had ever known.

Perhaps he had kept his girls too much away from the world. Except for their cousins, they had seen very little of other people. For that matter, they had never even been out of France! It was time that the three who were left to him should see something of the world. He would take them on a long trip through Italy and perhaps to Greece and the Holy Land. Those were the places he had planned to visit with his wife. But then she had died.

The next morning at Mass, the priest talked about a pilgrimage to Rome. It would take place in the fall, and the people of Lisieux were invited to join. This was just the way, thought Louis Martin, for the girls to begin their travels.

When he told them of his plan at dinner that day, there was great excitement. To think that they were to see Rome, and the Holy Father himself!

Thérèse thought, "The Holy Father's blessing will help me enter Carmel sooner."

But just then her father said, "We may be gone for quite a few months."

She did not know what to do, for such a plan could only cause further delay. That evening as they watched the sunset, she said to Céline, "Before we start for Rome, I must tell Father everything. If he knows how eager I am to enter Carmel, then he won't plan such a long trip."

Céline agreed sadly. "But it seems too bad. Poor Father", she said.

Thérèse turned away and began to weep. The two who were dearer to her than all others, the Infant Jesus and her father, were calling her—but to places so far apart! One, to the Carmel; the other, to the world! How could she please them both? Where would she ever find the courage to speak to her father?

One evening, when the two were alone in the garden, he saw there were tears in her eyes. "Why, Little Queen," he said, taking her hand, "what is troubling you?"

Then the whole story came tumbling out. For five long years she had wanted to enter Carmel. She had been silent, fearing that she would hurt him. But now she knew she must tell him, because she wanted to enter soon, very soon.

At the thought of losing her, Louis Martin rose from his chair and began to pace back and forth, brushing the tears from his eyes. Then he put his arm around her, and together they walked and talked for a long time. He understood. If this was God's will, he would not stand in Thérèse's way. As he had sacrificed his two oldest, he must now sacrifice his youngest. It was agreed that Thérèse would make the trip to Rome and enter Carmel as soon as possible after that.

At last Thérèse's dearest wish was coming true. She was very happy. The convent behind the high hedge would not really separate her from her father. It would only bring them closer together through prayer. But her new happiness was not to last long. For the prioress of the convent said that they could not accept one so young unless Father Delatroëtte, their superior, was willing. And he was very strict.

When Thérèse and her father went to see him, he greeted them coldly. "At fourteen, you are still only a child", he said. "No one so young can be allowed to enter the Carmel."

Now there was only one person in all France who could help Thérèse. That was the bishop of Bayeux. If he should consent, Father Delatroëtte would have to obey him. So Thérèse and her father went to Bayeux. The bishop was a kindly man and wanted to help Thérèse, for when he talked with her he knew that the Infant Jesus had really called her to Carmel.

But he said to her, "Because you are so young, I

wish to think longer about your entering Carmel. You are going to Rome with your good father. My friend, Father Révérony, will also be with the pilgrimage. While you are in Rome, I will try to send you a message through him."

Thérèse was most unhappy. She would have to wait for the answer until they got to Rome. But her father was thinking that, whatever the outcome, he would be happy for one long month, traveling about with his three daughters.

Then, only a few days before they were to leave, Léonie came to him. He guessed from her face what it was that she wanted to ask. "You too want to enter the Carmel!" he exclaimed.

"No, Father dear, not the Carmel," she replied, putting her arms about him. "For I am not good enough to lead so strict a life. But I have been writing to the Visitation Convent at Caen. They say that if I will come to them now, they will give me a trial. They are not certain about my health."

And indeed Léonie had not been well during the whole past year. Her work for the poor and the sick had worn her out.

"Well, dear," said her father, "I cannot stand in your way either, if that is what you want. But surely you will come to Rome with us first?"

Léonie looked very unhappy. "It seems that I must go now or wait for another six months. I should so much like to go now, Father!"

And because Léonie was twenty-four, her father felt that he should let her do as she wished. So he agreed, but with an aching heart. The desire for the convent was almost like an epidemic in his family! But he told himself not to be sad yet about Léonie. After all, it was only a trial. Perhaps she would soon be home with them again. If not, he would have only Céline left to him. Yet here was this young Charles from Alençon, who plainly was in love with her. He came from a fine family, and it would be a good match. Louis Martin sighed. How lonely it would be, when all of them were gone!

At last the day came when they would start for Rome. Léonie had left for Caen the day before. Victoire had been busy all week, preparing and packing the clothes of the two younger girls. Early that morning, Victoire, holding Tom by the collar, waved good-bye to them from the front door.

"It's terrible, not to be able to take Tom", said Thérèse.

"Well surely, you don't imagine that the Holy Father wants to see Tom!" exclaimed her father, teasingly. "And there's one thing certain. *You* may be allowed to enter the Carmel, but not Tom!"

The many people who came from different cities in France were to meet in Paris. From there they would go on to Rome together. Céline and Thérèse had a wonderful day in Paris with their father. He showed them all the sights, and of course they visited the Church of Our Lady of Victories, where so many prayers had gone up for Thérèse at the time she had almost died.

On the train the next day, they met the other people who were going on the pilgrimage to Rome. Louis Martin had found seats for his daughters near the windows, where they could see the great snowy Alps as they passed through Switzerland. Soon they were in Italy, where they stopped at many old cities to see the sights.

It was almost the middle of November when they reached Rome. A week would pass before they could see Pope Leo XIII. This would give them time to visit many of the famous places in Rome. But even the excitement of sightseeing could not make the time pass quickly for Thérèse.

Every day she waited hopefully for a message from the bishop. But whenever she met Father Révérony, he would shake his head. "I have had no word", he would say.

Thérèse became more and more discouraged. She was praying every day to Saint Peter—to all the great saints of Rome. Would the bishop say that she was too young? Would she have to wait more long years, as she had waited for the past five, to have her heart's desire? It seemed too much to bear. Just because she was young, others thought that she could not be a good Carmelite. She *could* be a good Carmelite, for she wanted to put her whole heart into it. "For love of the Infant Jesus", she kept repeating to herself.

The day at last came for their meeting with the Holy Father. No word had come from the bishop. Suddenly Thérèse knew what she must do. She must ask the Holy Father himself to let her enter Carmel! If he gave his consent, then no one—not Father Delatroëtte, not even the bishop himself—could stop her. When she told her father and Céline what she was going to do, they were amazed. But her father was proud of her courage. Céline asked if she would not be frightened—there would be so many people about. They would think it strange of her to ask such a question of the Pope.

"Oh yes, I shall be frightened", agreed Thérèse. "But I *must* do it. For I cannot go back to Lisieux without knowing!"

"But what will the Pope think?" asked Céline.

"He is a saintly man," said Thérèse, "and wants only to please the Infant Jesus. He will know that the Infant Jesus wants me to enter the Carmel, and he will surely give his consent!"

When the three Martins reached the Vatican, they found the other pilgrims gathered about Father Révérony.

"Remember," he was saying to them, "no one is to speak to the Pope. You are simply to kneel, one by one, at his feet, receive his blessing, and move on quickly."

Thérèse felt her heart flutter with fear. She *must* speak to the Pope! But if she did, then Father Révérony would be greatly displeased. And when he got home, he would surely tell the bishop. Then things would be harder than ever. They would say that she could not even be obedient. What chance then would she have of ever entering the Carmel?

Unhappily, she moved forward in the line, her father just in front of her and Céline just behind. Father Révérony was standing right next to the Pope's chair. "Oh, if he would only go away!" thought Thérèse. But there he stood, and as the pilgrims came forward, he announced the name of each to the Holy Father.

When her father knelt, Thérèse heard Father Révérony say, "Louis Martin has two daughters who are Carmelite nuns."

She saw the Pope smile and lean forward to give her father a special blessing. Now it was her turn. She dared not glance at Father Révérony. Trembling, she looked up into the Pope's kindly face.

Before she knew it, the words came pouring out. "Most Holy Father, please let me enter the Carmel as soon as I return to Lisieux!"

The Pope looked down at her in surprise. Then he smiled into her eyes. "Well, my child," he said, "if it should be the will of God, you will surely enter."

And then he blessed her. But Thérèse still knelt

there, looking up at him hopefully. This was not the answer she wanted. Someone took her sharply by the arm, raised her to her feet, and pushed her along the line. And now she was forced to move away. The tears streamed down her face.

The Holy Father had not granted her only wish. He had not seemed to understand that it was also the wish of the Infant Jesus. Carmel, Carmel—would it never be hers?

8

THE HIGH MOUNTAIN

A COLD WIND was blowing as Marie Guérin hurried up the hill leading to the Martins' home.
November was drawing to a close. The bushes and
trees in the garden, so green and thick in the summer, now seemed like thin, brown skeletons shaking
their fingers at her as she ran up the path. The Martins had just returned from their pilgrimage, and she
could not wait to see her cousin Thérèse.

Victoire opened the door, and at once Marie called out, "Thérèse! Thérèse! Where are you?"

There was a patter of feet on the floor above, and Thérèse flew down the stairs and threw her arms about her cousin. "Oh, Marie! So much to tell you!"

"Has the bishop given his consent?" asked Marie breathlessly.

The smile faded from Thérèse's face.

"No, oh, no," she sighed. "But come sit beside the fire, and I'll tell you everything."

Victoire brought them some hot tea. In a short time, Thérèse had told her cousin how she had waited in Rome for a message and how at the last she had spoken to the Holy Father himself.

"Oh, Thérèse, how did you ever dare?" asked Marie. "And was it not a mistake to displease Father Révérony?"

"Of course, but I was so sure that the Holy Father would make everything right", answered Thérèse unhappily. Then she brightened. "But do you know, I have a feeling that somehow he will."

"But Father Révérony has probably told the bishop that you disobeyed him!" said Marie. "I wonder that you could face him on the trip home."

"At first it was terrible", agreed Thérèse. "I was afraid to look at him and kept out of his way. All went well until we reached Assisi. Oh, Marie, it is so beautiful there! But I prayed so long to Saint Francis that when I ran out into the sunshine, all the seats in the carriages were full—except for *one* seat in *one* carriage. And can you guess whose carriage that was?"

"Father Révérony's", replied Marie promptly.

"Exactly", said Thérèse. "And I had to climb in. I was sure he would scold me. But instead, he smiled and talked pleasantly all the way!"

"Oh, then he has forgiven you!" exclaimed Marie.

"I hope so", said Thérèse. "And I hope that he will soon send the bishop's consent. He knows how anxious I am, and he knows that I will be fifteen in January."

"Why, your birthday is almost here!" exclaimed Marie. "We shall just have to go on praying for good news."

"Oh, please do", begged Thérèse, her eyes filling with tears.

It was hard to keep from crying these days. For the weeks dragged along, and still no word came from the bishop. Thérèse's father did everything he could to comfort her. One day at dinner he said, "It may be some time before we hear from the bishop. So, while we are waiting, what would you two think of a trip to the Holy Land? We could be there for Christmas. Think how wonderful that would be—to spend Christmas in the land of our Lord!"

Thérèse reached over and patted her father's hand. "Dear Father, you are always so good to us! But if you do not mind too much—and if Céline does not mind—may we not stay here a little longer? At any day, word may come."

But still the days dragged on, and there was no message.

Thérèse had made up her mind that hers would be a very sad birthday on January 2nd of the year 1888. When she was a little girl, she had always thought that the day after New Year's Day was a very happy time to have a birthday. A year was beginning again, bright and new. And always on January 2 it had seemed that she herself was beginning all over again. But this year it would be different, unless the bishop should send her the one birthday gift she desired more than all others. But there seemed little hope.

Aunt Céline had planned to make a round of calls upon her friends on the afternoon of New Year's Day. She wanted the Martin girls to go with her, for she was very proud of her nieces and liked to show them off. And Thérèse was becoming a little beauty, she thought to herself.

But when she mentioned the plan at Christmas, Thérèse had said, "Dear Aunt Céline, it is lovely of you. But would you mind terribly if I just stayed at home with Father that afternoon? I don't feel much like meeting people just now."

Céline said quickly to her aunt, "I should love to go with you and Marie! What time shall I be ready?"

Their aunt had gone off, happy that she would

have at least one of her pretty nieces with her that day.

When New Year's afternoon came, Céline danced down the stairs in her prettiest dress and sped into the room where her father and Thérèse were reading.

"I'm off to meet the world", she cried as she kissed each of them lightly on the cheek.

"You look as pretty as a rose, my dear", said her father. "Have a happy time. But be sure that it is your *aunt* who brings you home!"

"Who else would want to?" asked Céline, whisking out of the room.

"Who but Charles?" called Thérèse with a wink at her father.

"The sooner you go to the convent, the better", returned Céline as she flashed out the front door.

She had not been gone ten minutes before they heard the bell sound. Victoire went to the door and in a few moments entered the room, carrying a letter. "For Thérèse", she said. "It is from the Carmel! And brought by a special messenger!"

Thérèse's fingers trembled so that she could scarcely open the envelope. But as she read, her father saw a smile spread over her face. He knew at once that all was well.

"Father!" she cried, jumping up and running to him. "Look! It is from the prioress of the Carmel. She writes that the bishop has given his consent!"

And there it was, all written down in a charming letter from Mother Mary of Gonzaga. The bishop had written to her, asking her to tell Thérèse that he was quite willing for her to enter the convent, now that her fifteenth birthday was at hand. He left the time of her entry to the prioress. The only thing that lessened Thérèse's joy were the letter's final words.

"I should like, my dear, to welcome you to the Carmel right after Easter", wrote the prioress. "Just now, we go into a period of fasting that will not end until then. I think, in view of your youth, that it would be best if you joined us after this period."

"Oh, Father," cried Thérèse, "I don't mind the fasting! Reverend Mother does not understand. I'm entering the Carmel to *make* sacrifices."

Louis Martin put his arm about her. "Now dear," he said, "just be thankful to God for granting your prayer. And on the eve of your birthday! It is his way of wishing you a happy birthday."

Thérèse did not know whether to weep or to sing. She had waited so long! Now, at last, her prayers had been heard. She was to have her heart's desire. But yet she must wait another long three months. Only *she* knew how long those months would seem.

The prioress had closed her letter with these words: "Please come to see me, right after the New Year. We have many things to discuss."

The next day, her birthday, was one of the happiest Thérèse had ever known. She lost no time in telling her cousin Marie the good news. Marie was as delighted as Thérèse herself.

"Thérèse dear," she begged, "on the day that you go to see the reverend mother, please, please, take me with you!"

"Why, of course", said Thérèse. "Of course you may come with me."

When the day arrived for the interview at the convent behind the high hedge, Thérèse went in first to talk with the prioress. Her cousin waited outside in the hall.

After a half-hour had passed, Thérèse went to the door and called to Marie. Then she said to the prioress, "This is my cousin, Marie Guérin."

The prioress welcomed her kindly, and for a few moments the three talked of general things. Then the reverend mother turned to Thérèse. "By the way, my dear," she said, "I forgot to tell you that, when you come to us, you shall be called Sister Thérèse of the Child Jesus."

Thérèse and Marie looked at each other in astonishment. This was the very name that Thérèse had long ago chosen for herself. But she had told no one but Marie about it. It had remained a secret between them. Suddenly the two broke into smiles. For this seemed to be a sign that the Infant Jesus was pleased that Thérèse would soon enter the Carmel.

As they were leaving, the prioress turned to

Marie. "Come back someday and see me again", she said with a smile.

"Oh, indeed I shall, Reverend Mother!" exclaimed Marie.

Thérèse had noticed that her father seemed very tired and pale these days. Then came a morning when he did not appear for breakfast. The two girls rushed upstairs to his room and found him in bed, looking very ill. There was a strange twist to his cheek, and he spoke with difficulty.

Thérèse turned pale and dropped to her knees beside the bed. "Father dear, would you like to see the doctor?"

In his eyes she read that he would. At once Céline ran downstairs and sent Victoire off to find Dr. Notta. Thérèse stayed at her father's side and held his hand. She smiled bravely, but within her she felt sick with fear.

Later, after the doctor had made his examination, he said to the two girls, "Your father has suffered a slight stroke. If he is very careful, it may be a long time before he has another. But it is a warning. He must rest more and have good care."

Thérèse was miserable with worry. Now, only within a few months of her entry into Carmel, her beloved father had fallen into his first serious illness. Was this a sign that she should not enter the convent? Suppose he did not get better? Was not her place at her father's side? Céline alone could not take care of him. She, Thérèse, would be needed also. She went to Our Lady of the Smile.

"Dearest Mother," she prayed, "you asked your Son to cure me when I was very ill. And he did. Now, please, say the same prayer for my father. If he does not get well, I cannot please the Infant Jesus by becoming a Carmelite."

In a very short time, Louis Martin was much better.

Then one day a letter came from Léonie, written from the Visitation Convent. "I am coming home", she wrote. "I have been happy here, but the reverend mother does not think I am strong enough to go on with this life now. Later, if my health improves, I will be accepted here as a nun."

The household was delighted at the thought of having their Léonie with them again. Thérèse felt as though a great load had been lifted from her heart. Now, should her father fall ill again, there would be two daughters at home to look after him—Céline and Léonie. She could enter the Carmel with a free mind. Whatever happened, he would be lovingly cared for. And her prayers from the convent could help him far more than her prayers from the world.

The day had been set when she would enter the Carmel. It was to be April 9th of the year 1888. Just a few days before, Léonie arrived home. They were so happy to see her again, and Victoire cooked a very special dinner in her honor.

"Thérèse dear," Léonie whispered to her little sister, "are you sure you are strong enough to become a Carmelite? I thought I was strong enough to be a nun. Yet look what has happened to me! And you are so much younger."

Thérèse put her arms about her. "It will be all right, Léonie dear, for both of us—for you, later; for me, now. The Infant Jesus will give us the strength we need, if only we put all our trust in him."

Louis Martin had made up his mind that Thérèse's last evening at home would be a happy one. So her aunt and uncle and her cousin Marie were invited to a special dinner for her. Victoire outdid herself in preparing a delicious meal. Louis Martin had meant to be very cheerful at the table, but every time he looked at Thérèse, something choked in his throat. The Guérins also seemed very quiet. Céline thought that never in her life had she tried so hard to amuse everyone and to keep them from being sad. Through a great effort, she and Léonie managed to keep the talk and laughter going. Thérèse herself was torn between joy and tears.

Early the next morning, she ran out for a last look at her rose garden. But it still looked bleak, with only tiny shoots of green appearing here and there. In a few weeks, however, the roses would be glorious in their color and beauty. In God's garden, her cousin Marie was a rose. How well she would adorn the great home that would someday be hers! Joan of Arc had been a beautiful white lily.

"Little Jesus," she prayed, "I am only your smallest flower. But please accept me and make me grow for you in the garden of the Carmel."

She knew something about that garden. It grew on the slopes of a steep mountainside. For the Carmel had been named for Mount Carmel in Palestine—a holy mountain where, from earliest times, men had lived to be alone with God. It was steep and difficult to climb, but its heights led to the feet of God. Not all were strong enough to reach the top. But those who did found heaven waiting for them. She turned back toward the house, determined that she would climb that mountain and never falter until she had reached the top.

Soon she was sitting in the carriage, clasping her father's hand. How strong and kindly it felt! Léonie and Céline sat facing her. Victoire was standing at the door, wiping her eyes with a corner of her apron.

As Céline looked at Thérèse, she made a funny face and said, "I have heard that in the Carmel, if you are disobedient, they put live spiders in your bed."

Everyone laughed, for Thérèse had always had a great fear of spiders.

"Then I shall probably be eaten alive", declared Thérèse.

Louis Martin gave a last embrace to his Little Queen and turned away quickly. Thérèse passed through the door. She did not feel as if she were walking. It was as though she were floating just above the earth.

She had begun to climb the steep slopes of Mount Carmel. It took courage and a brave heart.

9

ROSES OF GLORY

IN THE CENTER of the convent was a garden and some leafy chestnut trees. This was the third garden Thérèse had known in her life, but how different it was from that of her babyhood in Alençon and that of her girlhood in Lisieux! The others had been gardens of play. This was to be a garden of prayer. Yet here were to bloom the most glorious roses she had ever grown for the Infant Jesus—the most glorious, but those with the sharpest thorns.

There were no thorns evident on the day of her arrival. She had been welcomed with open arms by the prioress and by her own two sisters, Marie and Pauline. She was a postulant, a newcomer begging for admission into the Carmelite Order. She must pass through a period of training before she could be accepted as a nun. Thérèse had known that the training would be hard. She was ready for that—but not quite ready for the hidden thorns that soon began to show themselves.

She had known that her greatest sacrifice would be to remain almost a stranger to her two beloved sisters while under the same roof. She could not fly to them for advice in her problems or for comfort when the thorns pricked deepest.

She had not been there many days before she realized that many of the nuns thought she was too young for the life of a Carmelite. For the Carmelite day was one of hard work and long prayer. Nor could she sleep the night through, for the night also was broken by prayer. Never had Thérèse felt so tired. But also never had she felt so happy or so much at peace.

Soon there came a day when she was told to sweep the cloisters. The broom was taller than she, but she held it firmly and put all her strength into the task. She told herself that she would sweep the cloisters cleaner than they had ever been swept before. At the end of an hour, weary and hot, she set the broom down and gazed at her work with pleasure. How clean everything looked!

But just then all the nuns filed past, with the prioress at their head. Suddenly the prioress stopped. Frowning at Thérèse, she pointed to a corner near the ceiling that Thérèse had not noticed.

Trembling, Thérèse looked up at the corner to which the prioress was pointing. To her horror, a giant cobweb dangled there.

"Sweep away that cobweb", said the prioress, "and be more careful in the future!"

Thérèse could feel all the nuns looking at her, and she thought she would die of shame. Now certainly all would consider her too young to be here. Perhaps, she thought, as she swept down the cobweb, they would send her home tomorrow!

But next day, as usual, the novice-mistress gave her more tasks to do. "From now on," she said, "you will weed the garden daily at four o'clock. And since you are to become Sister Thérèse of the Child Jesus, how would you like to take care of the shrine of the Infant Jesus?"

Thérèse flushed with pleasure. "Oh, I don't deserve it! But thank you", she exclaimed.

So from that day onward, Thérèse was the guardian of the shrine. Early every morning she hurried there with her duster and the flowers she had gathered in the garden. The shrine had never been so well cared for.

Within a week, a new task had been given her. The novice-mistress took her into the large dining room and said, "You are to sweep this room twice a day and help the others to set the tables."

Then she moved over to a small pantry just off the dining room. "And you are to keep this pantry clean", she said, as she opened the door.

As Thérèse looked at the many crowded shelves, she saw a large black spider run out from under the sugar jar. She drew back and gave a little scream.

"Surely you are not afraid of spiders?" asked the novice-mistress. "Why, they won't hurt you. They are God's creatures, too, and are useful. Think of Saint Francis. He loved all living things, and in return, they loved him. Were he here now, he would speak kindly to that creature and call him 'Brother Spider'."

"Oh", said Thérèse, still shivering.

"Now this will be a good way for you to imitate Saint Francis. You shall have charge of this pantry. Keep it in good order", she said as she closed the door.

"Yes, Mother", murmured Thérèse weakly, wondering how she would ever find the courage to clean those shelves. She remembered how Céline had teased her about the spiders in her bed, should she be disobedient. How had Céline known there would be spiders in the convent?

Troubled, again she took herself to the Infant Jesus.

"Little Jesus, I know your heavenly Father made the spiders. But they do frighten me. I never had a brother. And I wouldn't like to have a spider for one. Please help me not to scream in the pantry. Perhaps if I said 'Sister Spider', it would not be so hard."

Then Thérèse went straight back to the pantry, opened the door, and walked in alone. She was shaking all over, but she managed to move all the jars and clean each shelf. As she did so, many spiders ran out, but she noticed that they ran away from her. They were more afraid of her than she was of them. She did not want to kill them. They were God's creatures. But how should she send them away?

Then she noticed a window in the pantry and threw it open. Taking an empty box, she caught the spiders in it, one by one, and tossed each out of the window. After that, Thérèse was not afraid of the pantry any more.

Soon the novice-mistress came to see the shelves. "They are perfect", she said, smiling at Thérèse. "And I like your courage."

Shortly after Thérèse's sixteenth birthday, the prioress decided that she was now ready to become Sister Thérèse of the Child Jesus and to wear the clothes of a Carmelite nun. It would all happen at a beautiful ceremony at which Thérèse would enter the chapel dressed as a bride, to show that she belonged only to Jesus. Then she would leave, and, on her return, she would be dressed as a Carmelite nun.

Thérèse's father wanted her to have a lovely bridal dress for the first part of the ceremony. So he had a beautiful dress of white velvet made for her. When the box was brought to the convent and Thérèse opened it, she wept with happiness. For she saw that the dress was trimmed with delicate lace—the very lace her mother used to make. This was her father's way of making her feel that her mother also had a part in this wonderful day.

Louis Martin thought that he had never seen any-one so beautiful as Thérèse in her bridal dress. The Martin family was united again that day. The Guérins were also there, and Marie had never seen Thérèse look so happy. As Léonie saw her three sisters in Car-melite garb, she wondered wistfully how long it would be before she too would be dressed as a nun.

The Martin home seemed very lonely without Thérèse. Aunt Céline tried to amuse the two girls, but they took turns in going to the Guérin home so that their father would never be alone. He had not been well during the past few months, and again they were anxious about him.

One evening, Aunt Céline gave a dancing party and invited Charles, who was again in town. It was Léonie's turn to stay at home with her father.

The next morning at breakfast, Louis Martin asked Céline, "Well, my dear, did you have a happy time at the party last night?"

"Not very", answered Céline unexpectedly.

Léonie and her father looked startled.

"Why, how was that?" asked her father.

"Charles asked me to marry him", Céline answered.

"That does not surprise me", said her father. "And what did you say?"

"No, of course", answered Céline.

"Oh, you didn't!" cried Léonie.

"Charles would make a good husband", said her father thoughtfully.

"I suppose so—if one wanted a husband, that is", replied Céline. Then she broke into a sunny smile. "I told him that I had one man in my life now, my father. And that was quite enough, thank you!" She laughed gaily as she leaned over and kissed her father.

"But Céline," said Léonie, "Charles could give you everything!"

"I know", answered Céline. "But what do I want with a fine home and all those things? As long as I have Father and you and my painting—that's everything I want."

Later that day when Céline was alone in her room, finishing a picture, she thought that she had not been quite honest with them. There *was* something else she wanted, but it must wait. It must wait until her father no longer had need of her. She laid on the last colors and then stood aside to look at her work. Even she—and Céline was never pleased with her own work—had to admit that it was good. When the paint had dried, she would take it downstairs and give it to her father.

"My dear, you paint so beautifully!" exclaimed Louis Martin when she brought it to him the next day. "I'll tell you what we shall do, my Céline. We shall move to Paris, where you can study under the finest teachers. Someday you will be known as a great artist!"

It was plain that her father was delighted with the idea. Céline smiled and took his hand, but said nothing.

"Well, dear? Surely you would like that?" asked her father eagerly.

She sat down on a low stool beside him, still holding his hand. She had not wanted to tell him this. But now she must. "Father dear," she said gently, "it is a lovely thought. And I should be glad if it were not . . . if it were not for . . . " She could not finish the sentence.

"If it were not for what?" asked her puzzled father.

"Why, some day, dear Father, not now, of course—and it may be years away—I want to enter the Carmel. Then all the money you would have spent on me in Paris would have been wasted."

Louis Martin could not have been more surprised. "You too," he murmured, "my little Céline! Why, of all the five, you are the one I was sure would take a great place in the world."

"I want only Carmel. But not now," she said, "only later, when you no longer need me. For I shall never leave you, Father dear, as long as you live!"

Louis Martin was not ashamed of the tears that fell. He just sat there, holding her hand, and murmuring that it was a great honor the good God had paid his family. How blessed was a father who could claim five daughters as nuns! He sighed. All was well with his daughters. Now he could turn his thoughts toward heaven, where his Zélie awaited him. But it proved that three long years of suffering and illness were to pass before he could join her.

During those years, Thérèse was making her garden of roses beautiful in the convent behind the high hedge. Only God saw those roses. Those who moved about her saw only a very young nun who always seemed to be doing the most disagreeable tasks and was always smiling as she did them. Her poor father's illness weighed heavily upon her heart. Since she could not take care of him as Léonie and Céline were doing, she would find the convent's most difficult task and offer it to God as a prayer for her father. One evening in chapel, she saw that task at her elbow.

Sister Pierre had grown old in the convent and was

now so crippled with pain that she could not walk alone. When she sat, she had to have her foot on a special stool that was carried about for her wherever she went. Because of the pain, she was cross to everyone who came near. Someone had to help her from the chapel to the dining room. She frowned at Thérèse when the young nun approached.

"Mind how you handle that stool!" she exclaimed. "Carry it carefully."

Thérèse smiled and did as Sister Pierre wished. Then they started the long, slow walk to the dining room. Thérèse could make it on her own feet in five minutes. With Sister Pierre it took twenty. She had to grip the old nun around the waist to support her. As careful as she was, sometimes Sister Pierre stumbled.

"There! Now see what you've done. Oh, my poor back, my poor back!" she would cry.

When they finally reached the dining room, it took another five minutes to get Sister Pierre seated and her foot on the stool in just the proper way. Then her sleeves had to be turned back in just a certain manner. At this stage, Thérèse could have left her. But she noticed that Sister Pierre had trouble in cutting her food. So Thérèse stayed and cut it for her as it was set down. No one had ever done this service before for Sister Pierre. But she went on grumbling, and Thérèse only answered with her sweetest smile. When she finally reached her own place at table, the food was already cold. But she said nothing, and after that first evening, Sister Pierre would have no one but Thérèse help her from the chapel to the dining room.

Word reached Thérèse that dear Victoire had at last married her Léon. The Guérins had inherited the large home of which Marie had told Thérèse, and they had invited Louis Martin, Léonie, and Céline to spend the summer with them. How kind Marie would be to be her guests, thought Thérèse, smiling happily, and how well her lovely cousin would grace the beautiful home. Thérèse remembered that Marie had wanted to share the home with her. But no castle in the world could ever draw her from her beloved Carmel.

Pauline had recently been made prioress of the convent, and now she asked Thérèse to help the novice-mistress in training the novices. Thérèse did not feel equal to the task, but soon it was evident that the novices loved her and would do anything she asked.

About this time, the sisters in Carmel learned that Léonie had gone to Caen and had been admitted to the Visitation Convent. Her health had greatly improved, and as Louis Martin now had a nurse to look after him, as well as Céline, Léonie had felt free to go. Thérèse was happy for her. She was happy too when she read that her cousin Marie often sat with her father in the park and in the evenings played his favorite music for him. But it was Céline who now was with him constantly. And, little by little, she saw him failing. For more than a year, she scarcely ever left his side.

One Sunday morning toward the end of July in the year 1894, everyone knew that his end was near. As Céline bent over him, he looked up at her with a smile of gratitude and love. Then his eyes closed again, and he lay very still. At last he had gone to join his Zélie.

Only a few weeks later, Céline followed her three sisters into the Carmel. Sad as they were at their father's death, they were very glad to welcome her. Céline of the merry heart would make a wonderful Carmelite.

Less than a year later, the prioress one day sent for Thérèse.

"I have news that will please you", she said. "Our cousin Marie Guérin has asked to be admitted to the Carmel."

Thérèse's blue eyes opened wide.

"Marie, the rose, wishes to leave that beautiful home and live here in our poor convent?" she asked.

"She writes that she has wanted to come here ever since she talked with you at Trouville. Now it shall be your task to train her as a novice, although you are almost three years younger!"

It would not be hard to train *that* rose, thought Thérèse.

Now, except for Jeanne Guérin, who was married, and Léonie, who was in the convent at Caen, all the girls who had grown up together were united in the Carmel.

Thérèse had spent more than seven years in the convent behind the high hedge. Steadily, and with courage, she had been climbing the steep slopes of Mount Carmel. Her sacrifices had made a beautiful garden of roses for the Infant Jesus. She always thought first of him and then of others; never of herself. She delighted in taking the worst of everything. Her sandals were always patched, and her veil was worn thin and much mended.

She spent many hours every day praying for sinners all over the world and for all priests, especially the missionaries who were carrying our Lord's message to the far corners of the earth. She had longed to be a missionary and to die as a martyr for Christ. But for a very small flower in God's garden, that was not possible. Now the missionaries were writing to the Carmel in Lisieux, asking for prayers. Thérèse was asked to answer these letters. Soon she was writing to holy priests in China and other far places and offering prayers for them. Letters of thanks began to pour into the Carmel. They said that strange and wonderful things had happened because of her prayers.

One day her sister Pauline, the prioress, said to Thérèse, "I often recall our talks at home when you

were a little girl. You had chosen me as your second
mother, and I was pleased that you told me everything. I would like a record of your childhood and
of your search for the Infant Jesus. I wish you to
write it for me."

In obedience, Thérèse began carefully to set it all
down in writing, just as though she were writing a
letter to her "little mother".

That winter in Lisieux was a bitter one, and the
convent was poorly heated. Thérèse had never felt
so cold in all her life. The chilblains in her hands
were very painful. At night she lay shivering under a
thin blanket. But she said nothing. Suffering? Why,
this was nothing compared to what our Lord had
suffered or to what the martyrs had suffered. And she
had even fancied that she might be one of them!

She tried to hide the bad cough that now kept her
awake at night. As the months passed, she grew very
pale and thin. But she went right on with her duties.
To her sisters' questions, she replied that she felt well
enough and that they were not to spoil her.

One night, the cough was especially severe. In the
morning, she found a red stain on her handkerchief.
But she remained silent. Perhaps our Lord would
soon call her to his special garden. What a wonderful
day that would be! It seemed to her that, at twenty-
four, she had waited a very long time for heaven.

More than two years had passed since she had
begun to write the story of her childhood. The

prioress had liked it so well that she had asked Thérèse also to write about her life in the Carmel. She thought that the whole manuscript might be helpful in training the novices who knocked, year after year, at the convent door.

Thérèse had been very successful with the novices. She had always told them that the path up the steep mountain of Carmel was not a path of great deeds to set the world aflame, like those of Joan of Arc. It was a little, hidden path. It was one of small things, of obedience, and of secret sacrifices, made with patience, day after day. A mere child could follow it. In fact, she called it her own "little way".

The warm summer months came, but Thérèse's cough only grew worse. The prioress insisted that she be examined by a doctor. He knew at once that the young nun with the face of an angel had tuberculosis. Now she was forbidden to work very much. A chair was set out for her in the garden under the leafy chestnut trees. There she would sit with her pad and pencil, finishing her own story.

Not all the nuns realized that it was a saint who sat there. Thérèse had concealed her "little way" so well that many thought there was nothing unusual about her. But some of the wiser nuns now came every day to talk with her in the garden.

"What will you do when you reach heaven?" they asked her.

"Oh, I know what I shall do!" she would exclaim

happily. *"I shall spend my heaven in doing good upon earth."*

From where she sat, she could see the roses in the garden, nodding their lovely heads to every breeze that touched them. How beautiful they were! Would the unseen roses that she had grown for the Infant Jesus seem beautiful to him? From heaven, she would look down upon a world full of sin and full of sorrow. She prayed that our Lord would use some of her roses to help souls on earth to love him more.

She seemed now to hear him whisper that he would. So when the nuns again came to her, she said, *"After my death, I will let fall a shower of roses."*

Thérèse finished her book, which was later published as *The Story of a Soul*. The last act of obedience was done. She let the pencil fall.

"I had wanted to do such great things for you," she whispered to the Child Jesus, "like Joan of Arc. And like her, I wanted to save France. But this is such a *little* story."

On the evening of September 30, 1897, when Thérèse was not yet twenty-five, the long, steep ascent of Mount Carmel was done. She found herself at the feet of God. He leaned down and picked up the little flower and placed her right at the side of the tall lily, Joan.

Then there began to fall such a shower of blessings upon the earth as had scarcely ever been seen before. Everywhere, people who appealed to the Little

Flower in faith and love had their prayers answered. Sinners were converted, the sick were cured, the dying were saved, the work of the missions spread, and those who had never known God came to love Him. As Thérèse drew near to those who called to her, some of them could even smell the perfume of the roses.

Someone outside the Carmel happened to see some pages of *The Story of a Soul*. They were copied and recopied and soon were spread all over France. Within a year, all the pages had been printed and made into a book, and the books were being read all over the world.

When the first World War came, it seemed as though Thérèse's dream of saving France had come true. When France was all but conquered, the soldiers prayed to her. She came to them in the front trenches and on the battlefields. Many of them saw her there, in her Carmelite robe, as the shells burst through the night. She stood at the side of the wounded and the dying, and she comforted them. But she came not to the French soldiers alone. Many an American soldier was sure that he owed his life to her.

On the seventeenth of May of the year 1925, the Holy Father proclaimed to all the world that Sister Thérèse of the Child Jesus was a saint. She had been one of the youngest ever to find her way into God's beautiful garden of saints.